She had no idea
where she was

"Good, you're awake." Nico's voice brought her sharply around.

Saffron froze, acutely aware of her near nude state beneath the sheet. "Did you undress me?"

"You passed out....It isn't the first time," Nico mocked. "Although normally my women don't pass out on me."

"I'm not one of your women," she pointed out, "and I object to being classed as one."

"I wonder why? Is it because I get a response from you?"

"You don't!" She flung the words at him unthinkingly.

"You're trembling," he said.

"Because I hate you," she told him.

"You do?" Amusement glowed in his eyes, his mouth came down on hers. She moaned protestingly, straining to push him away. Against her will she felt a response stir deep inside her. "Nico...."

PENNY JORDAN
is also the author of these

Harlequin Presents

Many of these titles are available at your local bookseller.

For a free catalog listing all available Harlequin Romances
and Harlequin Presents, send your name and address to:

HARLEQUIN READER SERVICE
1440 South Priest Drive, Tempe, AZ 85281
Canadian address: Stratford, Ontario N5A 6W2

PENNY JORDAN

desire's captive

Harlequin Books

TORONTO • NEW YORK • LOS ANGELES • LONDON
AMSTERDAM • PARIS • SYDNEY • HAMBURG
STOCKHOLM • ATHENS • TOKYO • MILAN

Harlequin Presents first edition July 1983
ISBN 0-373-10609-2

Original hardcover edition published in 1983
by Mills & Boon Limited

CHAPTER ONE

'SAFFRON, my dear, you look wonderful—so like your mother!'

Behind the pride in her father's voice, Saffron caught the note of pain and understood the reasons for it.

For so long they had been estranged from one another—almost from the day of her mother's death when she was a schoolgirl of twelve and her father a busy, grief-stricken man of forty. Now that was over, miraculously they had found the way back to one another, and both of them treasured their new-found relationship.

'You approve then?' Saffron pirouetted in front of her father, the gauzy skirts of her dress fluttering round her body. The dress had been hideously expensive! She had bought it in London, especially for this occasion, which had been meant to herald the beginning of their long-awaited holiday together, but as he was the head of Wykeham Industries, Sir Richard's time was not entirely his own, and on the eve of their departure for Rome he had had to tell Saffron that it would be several days before he could join her at their villa in southern Italy.

'Most definitely,' Sir Richard assured her. 'And that's after being presented with the bill.' He marvelled at the change in her, from rebellious teenager to poised young woman; and it had happened almost overnight. He was so proud of this daughter, the child he had so nearly lost completely through his own bitterness following

his wife's death. He had forgotten that Saffron had
lost a mother too, and his guilt showed a little in
the concern with which he regarded her.

'I am sorry about our holiday,' he added, 'but
with luck I shouldn't need to be in San Francisco
for long. You'll enjoy yourself tonight at least.
Signor Veldini appears to have invited most of
Rome society to this party.'

'To impress you so that you'll agree to invest in
his business,' Saffron commented shrewdly. The
warm gold skin and dark red hair she had
inherited from her mother, coupled with a bone
structure a model would have envied, had resulted
in looks that had made her a photographer's
favourite almost all her teenage life. Add to the
sculptured perfection of her face, a perfect pocket
Venus-shaped body, and it was no wonder that his
daughter never lacked male escorts, Richard
Wykeham thought as he watched her.

The dress she had chosen for tonight's party
made her look as fragile and ethereal as a water-
nymph. A frown creased his forehead momentarily,
and seeing it Saffron smiled encouragingly.

'Don't worry,' she whispered as she took his
arm and he opened the door of her hotel room. 'I
won't let you down by sulking all evening because
you can't come with me—those days are gone.'

'They should never have been. If I hadn't been
so wrapped up in my business . . .'

'We made a pact not to dwell on the past,'
Saffron reminded him, the green depths of her eyes
momentarily shadowed as she remembered the
arid years of her adolescence and the pain of
losing her mother.

A limousine was waiting to ferry them to the
Veldinis' impressive villa in one of Rome's most

exclusive suburbs. Saffron had spoken no less than the truth when she had stated that Signor Veldini was hoping to persuade her father to invest in his company, but Richard Wykeham had a formidable reputation as an astute businessman and Saffron knew that it would take far more than a society party to convince him.

As they sped through the city she glanced at her father's face. She had been so looking forward to their holiday—their first together since the death of her mother. Her father had done his best. There had been a constant stream of mother-substitutes in the form of boarding schoolmistresses and housekeepers, but it hadn't been enough, and in an effort to make her father take notice of her she had involved herself in scrape after scrape. It was only within the last twelve months—since her twentieth birthday—that she had abandoned the wild set she had taken up with after leaving school—young adults like herself; the first generation offspring of self-made men, whose fathers had more money than time to spend on them and who themselves had been set apart from their parents by virtue of the public school education their parents had so proudly bought for them.

When would parents learn that children needed love, not money? Saffron wondered to herself. The greater part of her own rebellion had sprung not from any desire to share the wilder exploits of her set, but simply to draw her father's attention to her. It had taken the death of one of that set from drug abuse to shock her into the realisation of where her life was going, forcing her to attempt to reach out for her father one last time, and miraculously he had responded.

In the last twelve months there had been far

fewer aimless shopping sprees and hectic weekends of partying, and instead Saffron had discovered that she was becoming more and more involved in the welfare side of her father's business. His companies were known for their caring attitude towards their employees and, encouraged by her father, Saffron had become involved in a newly organised department designed to take this one step further, particularly to help the single-parent families amongst the employees, and Saffron had found this so absorbing that she had gradually let her old life slip away.

She knew her father was glad. If she did go out nowadays, it was normally for dinner, or to dance in a far more sedate nightclub than those she had previously frequented. Many of her old friends scoffed. Some of the boys in her crowd had been particularly mocking, reminding her of how she had always been the life and soul of the party, ready for any enterprise, always the first to agree to some impractical scheme.

But that was before she had realised the fine tightrope they were all walking. It was considered smart in her set to indulge in drinks and soft drugs, although something in Saffron had always made her hold back from experimenting herself— not from any moral objection but simply because she had seen the effect it had on others, and was reluctant to lose control of herself and her life in the same way—something she had a morbid fear of happening, which was probably why she had never become seriously involved with any of her dates. None of them knew, for instance, that she was still a virgin. Each thought that he was the only one not to enjoy a more intimate relationship with her. This was a belief she had fostered knowing that there was more safety for her in their fear of scorn at being the single failure than there ever would be in making public her innocence. Not even her father knew that the stories and rumours circulated about her in the gossip columns were just that, and somehow she found herself shy of broaching the subject with him. However, she was beginning to wonder if he hadn't started to suspect the truth. There had been a particularly amused glint in his eyes the previous weekend, for instance, when she had emerged from a taxi outside their London home, dexterously extricating herself from the expert and amorous embrace of the younger son of one of the French Ambassadorial staff. Jean-Paul was considered something of a catch in the circles in which she moved, but Sir Richard had been rather scathing about the young Frenchman's morals and abilities. 'Dilettante,' he had snorted, 'and not even particularly good at that!' And contrary to her previous practice, Saffron had found herself listening to and agreeing with her father's summing up.

Tonight, because he was going away and she wouldn't see him for some days, she wanted him to carry a good image of her. She had dressed carefully for the party; her beautiful Belinda Bellville dress, all shimmering white silk, and a froth of underskirts, the low-cut neckline trimmed with pink silk roses—and she was young enough to wear it—the diamonds which had been her mother's; tiny studs for her ears and a matching necklace and bracelet, both delicate and dainty. For the occasion she was wearing her hair up, in a soft chignon, tiny wisps of dark red hair caressing her neck. The silk rustled as her father helped her out of the car. The Veldinis' villa was ablaze with lights, and a liveried footman threw open the doors as they arrived.

'Very *fin-de-siècle*,' Sir Richard murmured in Saffron's ear as they climbed a shallow flight of marble stairs which led to an impressive marble-columned ballroom.

Signor Veldini had obviously been on the lookout for them. He reached the door at the same moment as they did, greeting Saffron's father with profuse and voluble exclamations of pleasure, before turning to admire Saffron.

'And this ravishing creature is your daughter? You are a very lucky man!'

His appreciation was entirely male and all Italian, and Saffron responded with a calm smile. A small movement several yards away caught her eye, and as she lifted her head she found herself looking straight up into the eyes of a tall, dark-haired man, standing alone. The dark hair and tanned skin proclaimed his Italian origins, but he was far taller than any other man in the room; topping even her father's six feet by a couple of inches, and even at this distance Saffron could see that his eyes were grey. She caught her breath as she saw the twinkle in them; as though he had read her mind when she had smiled to coolly and so reprovingly at Signor Veldini, and all at once her mood lightened. She had been feeling very depressed because her father could not travel on to southern Italy with her as they had planned. He would join her at the villa later when his business in San Francisco had been concluded, he had promised, but still she was disappointed.

'Paolo, will you not introduce us?'

She had been so absorbed in her thoughts that she hadn't realised the stranger had joined them; his words addressed to Signor Veldini but his eyes fixed firmly on Saffron's face.

At her side, she glimpsed her father's amused smile, and knew that she was blushing faintly.

'If the Signorina permits?' Signor Veldini begged formally, and when Saffron inclined her head, he placed his hand on the younger man's arm, drawing him forward slightly, so that Saffron's bare skin brushed the fabric of his evening jacket, evoking a trembling uncertainty that bemused her a little.

Even so she noticed that Signor Veldini had to glance up quite a long way to look into his companion's face, and that the grey eyes were slightly crinkled in amusement, as though he too saw through the Signor and his machinations to impress her father.

'Nico, you will be the envy of all our friends—they are all longing to be introduced to Miss Wykeham.'

'Saffron,' her father amended. 'And I am sure Signor. . . .' He paused and Signor Veldini filled in helpfully, 'Signor Doranti—Nico—has an English grandmother, which is why he speaks your language so well,' he explained to Saffron, while her father continued blandly, 'Signor Doranti will forgive me if I leave him with my daughter while you and I discuss this all important business you told me about, *signore*.'

'Only if you are absent long enough for me to dance with her,' Saffron heard Nico Doranti respond with a smile in his voice as well as his eyes. 'Unfortunately, Signor Veldini is in error,' he added as Sir Richard was eagerly escorted away by their host. 'I no longer have an English grand-mother—regrettably she died several years ago, but if I didn't cherish her memory before, I do so now, because it is my knowledge of her language and yours that enables me to steal a march on my fellow countrymen. Look at them,' he invited. 'They hate me.'

Saffron couldn't stop herself laughing. It was all so very absurd. And yet she liked him, felt drawn to him, despite his appalling flattery.

'Ah, that's better,' he said softly. 'When you walked in just now there were shadows in your eyes—such lovely eyes—the colour of malachite should never be clouded.'

He was astute, Saffron acknowledged; and very intensely male. She glanced at him. His profile possessed a sensual hardness that struck a chord within her; he was different—and dangerous, and something inside her thrilled to the knowledge; a purely feminine response to the fact that out of all the women in the room he had sought her out. Thick dark hair curled down over the collar of his dinner jacket. His hands while lean and tanned possessed none of the soft flaccidity she had grown used to among her London acquaintances. They were not the hands of a man used to idling.

'You have been in Rome long?' he ventured, adding softly, 'But no, you couldn't have been, or I would have heard of it. You are far too beautiful to come to Rome and remain unnoticed.'

'We arrived this morning,' Saffron replied demurely, 'and are leaving tomorrow. My father flies to San Francisco.'

'And you?'

Just for a moment desolation touched her. There was a lump in her throat and tears stung her eyes. She was being silly, she reminded herself, but she had set such store by this holiday, had been so looking forward to it.

'Come.' His fingers on her arm were warm and protective. 'There is a door over there which leads to the garden. We will walk through it, and you will be able to recover your equilibrium.

'Am I forgiven for upsetting you?' he murmured softly when they were outside.

Saffron nodded. He was so completely attuned to her mood and thoughts that she felt none of the hesitation or reserve she normally experienced, even with men she had known years.

The dark velvet richness of the Italian night with its scents and sighs embraced them. The gardens were formal—topiary walks and rose beds where Saffron could imagine fountains playing during the day.

The silly weakness she had experienced inside seemed to be exacerbated both by the night and Nico's sympathy, but even so she was surprised when he suddenly stopped, turning her towards him and tilting her chin.

'Tears?' A handkerchief was produced and used to dry the damp stains on her cheeks. 'May I ask why?'

'No real reason.' Her voice sounded shaky, but instead of feeling embarrassed she only felt an impulse to confide in him. 'It's just that my father and I were planning to holiday together—at our villa in southern Italy—and now he has to fly to San Francisco in the morning. It sounds silly, I know, but you see . . .'

'Yes?'

She had stumbled to a halt, embarrassed, but the soft persuasion of his voice encouraged her to go on.

'We've been on bad terms for some time,' she

explained simply, 'and now we've found one another again, and ...'

Her head drooped, long lashes fluttering down over her eyes to conceal her pain and doubt, astonished at her own confidence.

'And you fear perhaps that he does not wish after all to be with you?' Nico finished for her with quiet understanding.

His perspicacity shocked her. It seemed unreal that a stranger should know so much about her—see so much. It made her feel frighteningly vulnerable and yet overwhelmed with the relief of knowing that there was another human being who so perfectly understood her thoughts and feelings. The sensation was a strange one.

'It shocks you,' he guessed accurately, 'that I should so easily perceive that which you keep hidden from others, but there is a special chemistry between us; surely you feel it as I do?'

Did she? Her heart started to thump painfully against her breastbone. Was that the explanation for the strange awareness and sense of familiarity almost she had felt the moment she saw Nico? Or was she simply allowing herself to be carried away by her own mood and the undoubted magic of the evening? What did she know about him, after all?

What more did she need to know? an inner voice demanded; she knew how she felt when he looked at her, how her heart turned over at the sight of his ruggedly hewn masculine features, how her body had responded to his merest touch.

'Saffron.' Her name left his lips on a whisper, and tension coiled nervously through her muscles. She touched her lips with the tip of her tongue, unconsciously provocative. Sensuous appreciation flared in the smoky depths of Nico's eyes, and excitement spiralled dangerously through her. She closed her eyes instinctively, shocked by the sudden imagery of herself in Nico's arms, his mouth moving erotically over her own, the sensuality of the pictures flooding her brain shocking her breathless.

She swayed slightly, and felt the powerful bite of his fingers on her arms.

His lips brushed lightly across one damp cheek and then the other, and then he was putting her firmly from him, despite the parted invitation of her own lips. In the moonlight, Saffron could see the deep grooves on either side of his mouth. Against her will she experienced the faint stirrings of respect and even greater liking. How easy it would have been to dismiss him if he had reacted as so many of her escorts; subconsciously she had set him a test, and she was forced to admit he had passed it. Any other man would have taken advantage of her vulnerability, both emotional and physical, but Nico had known that the moment was not right for desire to flare to life between them. It was not desire she needed from him at this moment, but compassion and tenderness, and somehow he had known it. He frightened her a little, she recognised, with the ease with which he read her. Her physical response to him alone was enough to terrify her—something she had never experienced with any other man—without the added shock of the mental rapport which seemed to have sprung up between them and which did not need to rely on words.

'Come.' He spoke the word gratingly as though under duress, causing her nerve endings to shiver in response. 'We had best return before your papa sends out a search party.

'Where is this villa you go to?' he asked as they retraced their steps, and Saffron felt her heart soar with a joy she could never remember experiencing before.

She told him, briefly describing the area and the villa, and deliberately keeping her voice light, not forcing any invitation on him—somehow she felt they had gone beyond the need for that. She had lowered the barriers completely to him and there was no need to adopt the tricks or false pride normally expected in an exchange such as theirs.

When Nico eventually left her at her father's side, she felt bereft, and it showed in her expression. Richard Wykeham observed her with concern.

'It's all right,' she assured him, but her voice shook, and her eyes clung betrayingly to Nico's departing back.

She didn't see Nico again until she and her father were on the point of leaving, and then it was only the merest glimpse. He was standing at the side of an expensively fast Lancia, elbow resting on the open driver's door as he stared into the darkness. Just for a second in the powerful beam of their own car headlights Saffron saw his expression, and the shock was like a volt of electricity—stingingly painful. His face was drawn in lines of bleak anger, bitterness grooving his mouth; he was a stranger, and although he seemed to be looking straight at her, there was no recognition in that look.

It brought home to her the fact that they were strangers and that she knew nothing about his life; nothing about whatever had brought that look of inward and bitter brooding to his face.

*

Saffron had been at the villa for three days. The villa and surrounding countryside were beautiful but lonely, but strangely enough it wasn't her father who occupied most of her thoughts. It was Nico Doranti.

The couple who looked after the villa for her father were pleasant but in the main silent; neither of them was inclined to converse with her, and Saffron had decided to put her time in waiting for her father to the best use she could by topping up the tan she had got in Greece earlier in the year. She had given in to one of her friends' pleas to join them on a yachting holiday, cruising round the Greek islands; an idyllic-sounding holiday which, unfortunately, had turned out to be something of a nightmare. It was only when she joined the cruise at Athens that Saffron had discovered that everyone was paired off in couples and that she was expected to partner Jean-Paul. Events had gone from bad to worse, culminating in an appalling scene between herself and Jean-Paul one afternoon when the yacht was lying off the island of Corfu.

All the others had gone ashore and she had been sunbathing alone—or so she thought, until Jean-Paul crept up behind her and untied the strings of her bikini top. Since she had realised she wasn't alone her initial shocked reaction had been to whirl round, and it had been at that precise moment that a hovering photographer had seen his opportunity and snatched a picture of her from the quayside. Saffron had writhed in mortification to see it splashed all over the gossip columns days later. The grainy photograph had not shown clearly her shocked expression, but what it did show were the unmistakable curves of her breasts minus her bikini top. The usual innuendo-riddled caption had accompanied the photograph; she was holidaying with friends, including international playboy Jean-Paul Chalours, etc., etc.

Her father had pointed out that the photographer was only doing his job, but Saffron had felt besmirched by the incident, and it had proved the final straw in helping her to make a complete break with her old crowd. She had been surprised how little she had missed them; how content she had been in her father's company. She moved drowsily in the sunshine, her skin tanned a warm golden brown, contrasting with the minute emerald scraps that comprised her brief bikini. There was a matching jacket and wrap-round skirt on the sand beside her, and she sat up, swiftly fastening the skirt, as she stared out to sea. She would have hated Nico to have met her as the girl she had been. The other girls in her set would have drooled openly over him as they were wont; no doubt laughing shrilly in their attempts to focus his attention on them, the sharp, supposed to be witty, suggestive comments that were second nature falling from their glossed lips.

How would he have reacted to that photograph? Something told her that had she been spotted in such a compromising situation with him those photographs would never have reached the newspapers. But then Nico Doranti was hardly likely to steal up behind a girl and behave as childishly as Jean-Paul had done. For one thing he wouldn't need to, and for another, when Nico chose to make love to a woman it wouldn't be with one eye on the publicity he might gain. Saffron's face felt hot—nothing to do with the sun; a strange languor was creeping over her as she

contemplated how it would feel to be made love to
by Nico.

Long shadows were starting to creep across the
beach—a sign that the afternoon was dying. Soon
she would have to leave the beach and trudge up
the flight of stone steps cut in the cliff which led to
the villa perched at the top. She started to gather
up her belongings, glancing towards the cliffs and
freezing as she saw the lone male figure sauntering
towards her.

He was wearing ragged denim shorts, and a gold
medallion on a fine chain glinted in the sun before
disappearing into the dark tangle of body hair.

'Nico!'

His name left her lips on a startled whisper, her
eyes widening in unconscious appreciation of the
male litheness of his body. The shorts were well
worn and faded. They looked as though they had
once been jeans and had been cut down—the
genuine article, not some expensively fashioned
beachwear, and the frayed cuffs drew her eyes to
the solid muscle of his thighs. The sight of his
near-naked body had a powerful effect upon her
senses, heightened by the fact that he had been in
her thoughts almost constantly since their meeting.

'They told me up at the villa that I'd find you
down here,' he told her with a smile.

'You came to see *me*?' She hardly dared believe
it.

His eyes were mocking. 'Of course not! I can
think of at least a dozen other reasons why I
should drive hell for leather down here during the
middle of a particularly hectic working week. But
they'd all be lies,' he added softly, devastating her
by the way he looked at her, his glance
encompassing the feminine curves of her body.

'You surprise me,' he said at last, shifting his inspection to her flushed face and tremulously parted mouth. 'On a secluded beach like this I'd hardly have thought that——' he nodded towards her bikini and the skirt she had tied loosely round her waist, 'charming though it is—necessary.'

It was several seconds before the full implication of his words sank in, and when they did Saffron reached nervously for her sunglasses and slid them quickly on to her nose to conceal her expression. Had he genuinely expected to find her sunbathing in the nude when he made his way down those steps?

Suddenly awkward, she stepped away from him, appalled to discover how difficult she found it to think logically while he was there.

'Have you ... will you be staying long?' The question was disjointed, and she regretted the gaucheness of it the moment it was asked, but Nico seemed unconcerned.

'One day, perhaps two; I have booked into a hotel—if you can call it that in San Lorenzo, just down the coast. You know it?'

'Yes ... but you could have stayed here, at the villa.'

His eyebrows rose. 'Would your father approve of such intimacy?'

Again Saffron was shocked by her body's response to the picture he was painting; the two of them alone in the villa when Maria and her husband had returned to their own home in the evening. They could dine on the terrace that overlooked the sea, only the brilliance of the stars illuminating the scene, and afterwards ...

Her mouth had gone dry, her whole body responding with a sensuality that rocked the ground beneath her feet. She had never felt like this before. She glanced downwards distractedly, absently noticing her towel and suntan lotion still lying on the sand, acutely aware of the aroused firming of her nipples beneath the emerald cotton. And Nico was aware of it too. She could see his glance focusing briefly on the hollow between her breasts where the cotton twisted in a provocative bow, and for one delirious moment she almost willed him to untie the green fabric and replace it with the hard warmth of his hands. She shuddered deeply, perspiration breaking out on her upper lip. What was happening to her? Had Nico seen what she was thinking?

'Come, your Maria asked me to tell you that she is preparing dinner early tonight because she wishes to leave early. She mentioned that tomorrow is her day off and she intends to spend it with her daughter. I would suggest that we dine together, but,' his smile deepened the cleft in his chin, 'but it has been a long drive from Rome, and I am very much afraid I might disgrace myself and fall asleep. However, if I might be permitted to have breakfast with you, and then later, perhaps, we could go for a drive?'

Swallowing her disappointment, Saffron clung to the fact that he had driven all this way to see her, that he wanted to see her tomorrow, and managed an answering smile, bending to collect the rest of her belongings; a sharp exclamation leaving her lips as she stepped back on the jagged edge of a shell.

Pain lanced through her tender skin. She overbalanced, falling awkwardly, and was deftly caught by Nico.

His hands seemed to burn through the flesh of

her back, spread palm to fingertip against her skin as he steadied her.

'What happened?' He frowned and she shook her head.

'I stood on a shell—nothing much.'

'Let me see.'

He dropped on his haunches beside her, lifting her injured foot, so that she was forced to balance herself by gripping his shoulders. His skin had the taut sensuality of raw silk; the muscles it cloaked were supple. Saffron had to quell her desire to run her fingers over his shoulders and back. It would be like stroking the pelt of a jungle cat, she thought hazily, and just as dangerous. She glanced down, observing the dark head, and the deftness of the fingers exploring her injured foot.

'It looks okay,' Nico pronounced. 'It's bleeding quite freely, and as long as you wash and cleanse it thoroughly when you get back to the villa there shouldn't be any complications. I can't see any pieces of shell in it. Still, best to be sure.'

Before she realised what was happening Saffron felt the warmth of his mouth against her foot. Lean fingers curled round her ankle, and the feeling uncoiling inside her as Nico used his tongue to cleanse the small cut was like nothing she had ever experienced before. Who would have thought that the steady brush of his tongue against her skin could be so erotic?

'Saffron?'

Nico raised his head, his hand stroking upwards from her ankle, an expression in his eyes that sent her pulses hammering with answering desire. And then he was on his feet and she was in his arms, her lips parting eagerly for the hot possession of his kiss. His hand found the curve of her spine and caressed it, tracing its length, his mouth making hungry demands on her own. She was weightless, pure plastic to be moulded and re-formed as he wished, conscious of the fierce body heat he was generating, the need to press closer to the male hardness of his thighs.

When he released her it was like losing part of herself, and incredibly Saffron knew that if he had suggested there and then that they make love she wouldn't have made the slightest protest. She wanted him to make love to her, had wanted it, she now acknowledged, from the first moment she saw him. Nico wasn't like a stranger. In some compulsive way it was as though she had known him before; as though she had been searching through a millenium of time to find him; her senses recognised and welcomed him in a way her mind couldn't come to terms with. She wanted to tell him about it to ask him if he felt the same, but she was too shy.

He released her, steadying her and gravely handing her her things.

'Ciao,' he said softly. 'Don't forget, breakfast tomorrow. Something tells me you always look extremely attractive dispensing orange juice and coffee.'

There was a hint of mockery in his voice and Saffron wondered if he thought she was in the habit of breakfasting with men—with lovers, but surely if that was the case he would not have demurred about staying at the villa. Saffron knew he wanted her; and she also knew Italian men— very male, aggressively macho, and yet Nico was treating her with all the delicacy he might afford a piece of exquisite china; and she was enjoying it. She loved his reticence almost as much as she loved the sleek masculinity of him; the passion she suspected slumbered beneath the outward control. She obviously meant more to him than a mere one-night stand.

She longed to be able to communicate to him her joy that this should be so; the dizzying pleasure of knowing that he saw her as a person, not simply her father's daughter. But then he already knew how she felt, she thought on a soft sigh; how could he fail to do so? She had seen it in the quizzical smile he had given her, had felt it in the pressure of his mouth against hers.

Her heart full of dreams, she turned towards the villa, already looking forward to the morning.

CHAPTER TWO

WHEN she woke up, for the first time since her arrival at the villa Saffron felt a brief tingle of excitement; of anticipation for the coming day.

She showered swiftly, donning a white tee-shirt and a pair of khaki jeans, finding a clean bikini and matching towelling cover-up which she rolled into a towel and placed in the canvas rollbag that matched her jeans.

She had no idea what Nico's plans for the day might include, but she was not going to be caught out if he suggested stopping somewhere for a swim. She was aware that a less inhibited girl would probably not have worried about a bikini—certainly she couldn't think of anyone among her old crowd who would have been anything other than delighted to display their bodies in front of Nico Doranti.

With impeccable timing he arrived just as Maria was carrying breakfast out on to the terrace. Saffron heard the car and walked through the villa to the front door. As she opened it Nico was emerging from the driver's seat of a scarlet Mercedes convertible. In those moments before he saw her he looked almost withdrawn, the black knit shirt he was wearing stretching to mould his body as he bent to retrieve the car keys. Black jeans moulded the contours of his thighs—a casual outfit, not specifically designed to attract, and yet she was intensely aware of him; of the bronzed vee of flesh in the opening of his shirt, the gold

medallion nestling against his chest, the rugged
power of the indolently lean male body as he came
towards her, checking suddenly as he became
aware of her presence. His expression was
immediately transformed, the grimness banished
and purely male appreciation taking its place.

'If I'd known you look so good in the morning,
nothing would have persuaded me to return to my
hotel last night,' he drawled as he caught up with
her, curving an arm round her shoulders and
bending his head to obliterate the morning sun as
he kissed her lightly. Saffron wondered if he was
as intensely aware of the scent of her perfume as
she was of his cologne. He smelled clean and
masculine, and she had an overwhelming desire to
place her lips against the tanned column of his
throat.

'Breakfast is ready,' she told him huskily, her
lips still tingling from the brief contact with his.
'You timed it just right.'

'That depends.' He gave her a stunningly
comprehensive oblique glance that sent her pulses
racing. 'Personally, I wouldn't have minded at all
arriving a little too early, and discovering you like
Sleeping Beauty still slumbering, awaiting the
Prince's kiss.'

It was ridiculous to be so affected by his verbal
lovemaking. She had experienced it often enough
in the past without response, why should Nico be
so different? She didn't know. All she did know
was that the thought of him in her bedroom was
creating the most erotic pictures in her mind, and
she hurriedly tried to dispel them as she led him
through the villa and out on to the terrace.

She was glad she had taken such trouble with
the breakfast table when she saw him glance at it.

The newly warmed rolls lay in a golden heap in the basket; the small dish of apricot jam in the pretty green dish she had bought to match the pale green cabbage rose pottery they used in the villa making an attractive splash of colour against the buttercup yellow tablecloth.

They might almost have been a placidly married couple of longstanding, Saffron reflected half an hour later as she poured Nico a second cup of coffee. He was leaning back, relaxing in his chair as he studied the view from the terrace.

'What exactly are your plans for the day?' Saffron questioned, colouring faintly as she saw the way he studied her. 'I mean, should I make up some lunch for us or . . .'

'By all means, if it isn't too much trouble, although I must confess that right now, food is the last thing on my mind.'

Excusing herself to clear away their breakfast things and stack them in the dishwasher, Saffron left him alone in the main *sala*.

'Saffron.'

She hadn't heard him come into the kitchen and she nearly dropped the knife she was using to slice through rolls before she buttered them.

When she glanced up the expression in his eyes puzzled her. He looked preoccupied, as though he had far more on his mind than a day out.

'Perhaps this isn't such a good idea.'

He had his back to her, for which she was grateful, because it meant that he couldn't see the humiliated pain in her eyes. What did he mean? Was he having second thoughts about wanting to spend the day with her? Had he discovered that she wasn't after all the girl he had thought her in Rome?

'If you say so.' She managed to make her voice sound calm and indifferent. 'Although somehow I wouldn't have thought last-minute doubts were your style.'

Suddenly they were strangers and her last few words were designed to taunt and hurt. She saw his face change and knew with a shock that they were on the verge of a quarrel; a sudden black cloud in a hitherto blue sky.

'Obviously they aren't yours.' There was a hardness about the words that chilled her. 'Do you always make up your mind so impulsively about people—or is it only men?'

He had hit to hurt and had succeeded. How could she tell him now that she had never responded to anyone as instinctively as she had to him?

He walked back into the *sala* and Saffron followed him, knowing that the day was spoiled.

'I think we'd better call today off,' Nico began, suddenly pausing in front of a framed photograph on one of the tables. It depicted Saffron with her father, and one of her father's oldest friends. Nico was staring at it with a fixity that puzzled her, his eyes and mouth tautly bleak.

'An old friend of my father's,' Saffron told him. 'He . . . he died last year.' Her voice faltered and she bit hard on her lip. She hadn't known John Hunter all that well, although he and her father had been friends for many years, but she still found it painful to talk about his death. He had been a kidnap victim, and his subsequent death at the hands of his kidnappers had made headline news. Even now Saffron found it hard to shake off the sick horror that crawled through her veins as she dwelt on his ordeal. She had never even told her father about her own almost pathological fear of being kidnapped. Some people were terrified by spiders, she told herself flippantly; her phobia was kidnappers.

She suspected it stemmed from her mother's death. She had been at boarding school when it had happened and had known nothing. The arrival of two strangers, who she later discovered were her father's secretary and personal assistant, who whisked her away from school without explanation and then proceeded to tell her of her mother's death, had left a scar that had never completely healed.

'He was kidnapped by terrorists,' she forced herself to say, as though by speaking the dread word she could overcome her fear.

'Tragic.' Nico sounded as though he meant it, and for a split second Saffron found herself reliving her father's grief and the sharp resurrection of her own phobia, but she quelled it swiftly with a flippant, 'Oh, I don't know—isn't it everyone's private sexual fantasy?'

It was the sort of flip statement expected among her crowd and Saffron had often used them defensively in the past, not caring about the conclusions her companions would draw, but now she did care, and she bitterly wished the seemingly callous statement unuttered when she saw the look in Nico's eyes.

'Nico?' Her voice and eyes pleaded with him to understand, begged for the forgiveness her pride would not allow her to ask for, and miraculously his expression changed, a smile soothing away the frown and with it the harsh bitterness that had seemed so alien to his character.

'I think I must have got out of my bed on the

wrong side this morning.' His mouth twisted wryly. 'Or perhaps the problem is that it wasn't the right bed.' He glanced at his watch. 'How long will it take you to finish getting ready?'

No reference to the fact that ten minutes ago he had been on the point of cancelling their outing, but Saffron was too delirious with joy to mention it.

'Ten minutes,' she promised, and was as good as her word, watching with steadily escalating excitement as Nico stowed the picnic basket away in the boot of the Mercedes, and opened the passenger door for her to climb in.

They had the road almost entirely to themselves. Saffron relaxed back into her seat, enjoying the teasing caress of the breeze as it tangled her curls, breathing the hot, sensual scent of the countryside drowsing in the midsummer heat. They passed olive groves with trees so gnarled and ancient it wasn't hard to believe that they had probably been old when the Roman legions tramped these roads.

They were high up in the hills behind the villa. Below them the sea shone deep azure blue, merging into the distant skyline in misty lilac. Saffron sat with her knees hunched under her chin, aware of the heat of the sun as it beat down on to her shoulders. Half an hour ago Nico had pulled off the road in this beautiful, strangely desolate spot. Now he was lying at her side on the thin grass watching the sky. A pleasant breeze stirred the heated air. She ought to have been feeling pleasurably relaxed after the meal they had just shared, but she wasn't. Tension coiled her stomach like an over-wound spring, her body so intensely aware of the man beside her that she could sense his every movement without even looking at him.

He had removed the jeans and shirt he had worn
for driving and lay on his back, and Saffron
berated herself for not having followed his
example and donned her swimwear beneath her
tee-shirt and jeans. But Nico's brief trunks did
little to conceal his masculinity, and she forced
herself not to give in to the impulse to let her
glance wander at will over his body. She could
always go and change. There was no one to see
except Nico. As though he read her thoughts he
suggested lazily,

'Why don't you go and change?'

She wanted to, so why was she holding back?
What was this strange selfconsciousness that made
her reluctant to expose herself to Nico in the brief
triangles of her bikini?

'You are looking as though you were a
Christian maiden who preferred being thrown to
the lions to exchanging her virtue for the embrace
of her Roman captor. It is a novel experience,' he
continued lightly, levering himself up on one elbow
to study her. Dark eyelashes swept protectively
across her eyes, anxious to conceal her expression
from his probing glance, fearful that he would
read in her eyes the secret of her virginity. Why,
when she had never felt burdened by it before, did
she suddenly long for the experience and ex-
pediency of her peers? If only she had some
practical sexual knowledge to fall back on, to tell
her how to react.

'Why is innocence always such a lure to the men
who witness it? When I look at you now, I find it
hard to imagine any man other than myself has so
much as touched your lips.' Nico's expression
changed, hardening, his muttered, 'I must be
losing my grip?' lost as he leaned over her,

imprisoning her with his body, his voice thick and
unsteady as he said against her lips, 'Something
tells me I'm going to regret this, but right now I
can't think past the aching in my gut, that reminds
me I'm a male animal first, and a thinking human
being a very poor second. What is it those soft
eyes are begging for when they look at me so?
Reprieve? Or this?'

Saffron had known the first time she saw him
that he was a man who knew all there was to know
about the female sex, but he seemed to have
misjudged her badly, because the ferocious
pressure of his mouth, the desire he made no
attempt to temper, frightened rather than aroused
her. Deep down inside him she sensed a bitter
anger, an inner rage that drowned out seduction
and sensitivity and left only a raw need that even
she, inexperienced though she was, knew he had
not meant to betray. Why? she asked herself
numbly, frozen beneath his body, terrified by the
emotions she sensed churning through him. She
struggled to break free, panic tensing her muscles,
her mind and body crying out to her that she had
been a fool to allow herself to be alone with him.
What did she know of him after all? What if she
had merely imagined that rapport which had
seemed to make conventional preliminaries between them unnecessary?

As though he sensed the direction of her
thoughts the harsh pressure of Nico's mouth
suddenly relaxed. He murmured an apology
against her ear, stilling her frantic movements with
the sensual caress of his hand stroking over her
body.

'Forgive me, *cara*. I was too impulsive, my
desire for you too intense . . .'

Despite his words and the look in his eyes, Saffron had the momentary impression that he was playing a part, mouthing words he did not feel, but it died almost the instant it was born as his hand pushed aside the thin barrier of her tee-shirt, cupping the rounded softness of her breast, his lips brushing tantalising over hers, with none of the angry pressure of before.

Perhaps she had imagined his anger, she thought hazily, perhaps it had just been fostered by desire. She knew so little of the emotions which drove men, and he was obviously not a man used to denying his sexuality.

Her body's responsiveness to him frightened her, and she tried to wriggle away. 'We ought to be going,' she murmured shakily. 'I . . .'

Nico glanced at his watch and then seemed to search the scenery; the deserted sky and equally deserted road.

'Not yet,' he said softly. And when Saffron continued to protest he ignored her, simply bending his head and touching his lips to the warm valley he had exposed between her breasts, his touch making her toes curl in mute protest, her breath catching on a wave of shocked pleasure.

His fingers pushed aside the flimsy lace cups of her bra, savouring breasts which Saffron knew were surprisingly voluptuous in view of the slenderness of her body, and now they seemed more voluptuous than ever, her nipples hardening against his palms as pleasure shuddered through her.

'Nico . . .' His name left her lips on a tortured breath.

'I know,' he agreed huskily. 'Not here . . . but you make it very hard for me—very hard,' he reiterated throatily as his lips moved provocatively against the aroused peak of her breast, stroking it lightly and then stopping as he felt the shudder she was powerless to control. Her face had gone paper-white with the strength of her emotions; the shock of experiencing such a stomach clenching intensity of pleasure. She wanted to tangle her fingers in his hair and hold him captive against her body, but shyness and inexperience held her aloof, and then Nico was on his feet, pulling her with him, straightening her tee-shirt and motioning her towards the car.

She hadn't time to protest, and then, as she waited for him in the Mercedes, she realised that his hearing, more acute than hers, must have caught the approach of the battered Land Rover that came lumbering down the hill towards them.

It rolled to a halt and three people jumped out; two men and a girl, all dressed casually in a uniform of grubby jeans and sweat-shirts, and all of them carrying shoulder-hung machine-guns which were pointed in her direction.

Feeling as though she had suddenly strayed into a nightmare, Saffron watched helplessly as they advanced towards her. Behind her she heard Nico move, and a wave of relief swamped her to know that she wasn't alone. She turned towards him, sobbing his name.

'Get out of the car!'

It was the female member of the gang who issued the curt instructions, the heavily accented words just about penetrating the fog of terror engulfing Saffron.

'Nico . . .' She murmured his name as though it were an incantation against evil, helplessly appealing to him, her eyes widening in stunned disbelief as she saw his stony expression, and heard him say bleakly, 'Do as she says, Saffron.'

'But .. .' Couldn't he see that if she left the protection of the car she would be that much more vulnerable? The unkind laughter of the girl with the gun as she looked from Saffron's pale, distressed face to Nico's blank, frozen mask of rejection hurt as it grazed over Saffron's jarred nerves.

'Look at her!' the girl taunted. 'Even now she can't believe it. You must have done an excellent job of persuading her to accept you, Nico. Even now she cannot see the truth. Little fool!' she mocked Saffron, smiling evilly. 'Nico is one of us. He will not help you.'

Saffron looked at the taut aloof mask of Nico's face and knew sickeningly that it was true. He turned his head, cold grey eyes sweeping every vulnerable feature, and she knew with dreadful clarity that it had all been planned—every tiny last detail; every word; every caress, and she, like the fool she was, had fallen for it. And not just fallen for it, but woven stupidly sentimental dreams around him; deluded herself into believing that something rare and precious existed between them. Her head swam as she remembered how close she had come to giving herself to him. Thank heavens she had been spared that final humiliation! She pictured him and this bitter, olive-skinned girl with the hard brown eyes laughing over her lost virginity, her misplaced trust and adoration, and she reached blindly for the door handle, stumbling from the car in a daze. She stumbled on a sharp flinty stone, and would have fallen if Nico hadn't grasped her arm, but she shook him away with a gesture of bitter loathing, masking the pain aching through her, using the agony of his deception to transmute pain into anger.

Her low, husky, 'Don't touch me,' vibrated with horror and despair, and again the girl laughed mockingly. 'Ah, Nico,' she said contemptuously, 'you have spoiled all her pretty dreams. She thought you wanted her for herself, but in reality all you wanted was her father's money. How quickly do you think he will pay the ransom?' she continued. 'He had better not take too long, Rome badly need funds if we are to buy the equipment we need to . . .'

She broke off, gasping with mingled anger and pain as Nico left Saffron's side to grasp her wrist, swinging her round to face him as he said in a cold, even voice, 'Guard you tongue, Olivia!' His warning glance encompassed both her and Saffron, and Saffron felt her blood turn to ice water in her veins as Olivia tossed her head and remarked callously, 'What for? There are ways of making sure your little friend never gets to repeat anything she overhears, or have you lost your dedication to our cause, my friend? This is the second day we have made a rendezvous here.'

Nico's shrugged, 'I was delayed,' obviously didn't please her, and her thick dark eyebrows snapped together in a frown, her voice dangerous as she looked at Saffron. 'By that?' she demanded angrily. 'Nico . . .'

'I was delayed in Rome,' Nico elaborated, his face tightening as he rounded on her, saying softly, 'Try to remember that I am in charge here, Olivia, and that it is not for you to question my actions. Now, get the girl into the Land Rover, we have already spent too long here.'

'Come.' The muzzle of the machine-gun rested

in the vee of Saffron's tee-shirt. 'Pretty but soft,' Olivia commented, lips drawn back over sharp small teeth. 'Look how she shakes! This gun is very sensitive,' she told Saffron. 'The trembling of your body is enough to . . .'

'She is no use to us dead, Olivia,' Nico pointed out with deadly calm. He had changed so much Saffron barely recognised him. Gone was the indolence, the warm smile and easy charm, and in its place was a forbidding menace that struck a chill right through her bones. His features might have been cast in bronze, every movement weighed, every thought calculated.

'Not dead, perhaps,' Olivia agreed, gloating over Saffron's pale face, 'but her *papa* will still pay well for his daughter, even if we mutilate her a little. You did well to choose her, Nico, let us just hope for her sake that her father cares as much for her as you say. We have read about you in the papers, Saffron Wykeham,' she told Saffron, 'of your affairs and your father's money. We heard you were coming to Italy and laid our plans carefully. Nico told us it would not be hard for him to gain your trust; you have a weakness for handsome men.'

'Stop wasting time, Olivia,' Nico instructed. 'Get her back to the farm. I have to take the Mercedes back, and send the telex off to her father. We should see results pretty quickly. Now remember, when you get up to the farm everything should appear normal. It's bound to be checked out.'

'When will you be back?'

Saffron saw his eyebrows rise at the aggression in Olivia's possessive question.

'I don't know. It all depends how long it takes.'

'And her?' Olivia demanded, jerking her gun in Saffron's direction.

'Just stick to the plan,' Nico told her. 'No rough stuff, there's no point . . .'

'Because you don't want anything to spoil her soft skin?'

Suddenly Saffron realised that Olivia was jealous of her. What was the other girl's relationship with Nico? Were they lovers? The twisting pain in her stomach stunned her. Surely the knowledge of his deceit should have killed for ever whatever she had felt for Nico. It had done so, she assured herself fiercely; the pain she felt was the result of her shock.

'Her skin is of no interest to me apart from the price we can put on it,' Nico said carelessly. 'You should know that. You should also know that we're going to have to supply proof to her father that she's still alive, which is why I don't want a hair on her head harmed—at least not for now. I'll take the shots of her when I get back.' He glanced at the heavy gold watch he was wearing, and Saffron felt physically sick, realising how he had come by the money to afford such luxuries. She had ceased to exist for him as a person, if indeed she had ever done so; she was simply a marketable commodity.

His last words for Saffron as he turned away leaving her with her three armed guards were, 'Don't be tempted into doing anything rash. Olivia has orders to shoot if you do.'

'And not to kill,' Olivia warned her, grinning viciously. 'You'll look one hell of a lot less attractive with shattered knee-caps.'

It was impossible for Saffron to hold back her shudder of horror. Olivia's cruel laughter was

drowned out by the Mercedes' engine firing, the
paintwork flashing briefly in the sun before it
disappeared in the direction she had driven with
Nico such a short time ago.

It was the realisation of all her worst nightmares;
a descent to hell itself, with every nerve in her
body screaming in mindless panic as she fought
against her desire to turn and run, knowing that to
do so would be to invite Olivia's gleeful retaliation.

As she stood there in the hot sun, all her
tentative awakening emotions were gripped with
the frost of reality. Desire and burgeoning love
had been crushed by bitterness and a burning
desire for revenge; not so much because she had
been kidnapped, Saffron realised, but because of
the way it had been accomplished; the ease with
which Nico had insinuated himself into her life,
her vulnerability towards him. He had used her,
coldly, calculatingly and callously, and she would
make him pay for that if she spent the last drop of
her life's blood in doing so. A raging thirst for
revenge filled her, blotting out fear and panic, and
making her strong enough to face the barrage of
those three cold faces and three machine-guns with
pride and calm.

Her anger burned with the death touch of
unyielding ice, enabling her to clarify her thoughts,
and use the adrenalin pumping through her veins
to think swiftly and clearly. Her father was a
millionaire and that fact was well publicised,
which, presumably, was why they had made her
their prey, but most of his wealth was tied up in
his business, and even if he could raise whatever
ransom was demanded, Saffron had severe doubts
that she would ever be set free. She had already
read her fate in the implacable eyes of her

kidnappers; how many victims suffering exactly her situation had ever been released? Look at her father's close friend. He had been kidnapped and then murdered. She was faced with two choices; either she could give in to the panic she had battened down inside herself and become a grovelling, pleading object; or she could devote her last ounce of stamina, all her mental and physical reserves in trying to outwit her captors. The same instincts which had raised her father from relative obscurity to the position he held today surfaced in Saffron; the age-old need for survival pumped urgently through her bloodstream, and without conscious volition her decision was made. As she numbly followed the direction Olivia indicated with her gun the words of an old saw floated into her mind, 'Living well is the best revenge,' but in her case simply living would be her revenge, and she would cling to that thought with every breath she drew. Somehow, she didn't know how yet, she was going to live and she was going to bring to justice those who had perpetuated this crime against her; and Nico ... Revenge was a heady wine and she had drunk deeply of it; deeply enough to overcome her fear, and her mind worked feverishly as she sought some avenue of escape, striving to ignore the dangerous silence and the two guns at her back as Olivia led the way to the dusty Land Rover.

CHAPTER THREE

'In,' she ordered Saffron curtly. The muzzle of the machine-gun pressed coldly against her spine, but Saffron refused to give way to the terror threatening to surge over her, sesnsing that this was exactly what Olivia was waiting for.

Of the two men, the taller watched her impassively as she struggled into the Land Rover, but it was the smaller, swarthier of the two who made Saffron shudder as she saw the way his eyes roamed hotly over her body.

'Remember what Nico said,' Olivia instructed as she swung herself into the Land Rover. 'When we get back to the farm everything must appear as normal.'

'Nico!' The swarthier of the two men spat noisesomely. '*Dio*, who is Nico to give us orders? Always before we have worked on our own.'

The complaint had an air of repetition, confirmed when Saffron heard Olivia respond curtly, 'That was before. We have orders now from Rome. Nico is in charge. Wasn't he the one to suggest this?' she added defensively. 'It will make us more money than . . .'

'Money—ah yes, we are always in need of that,' the taller of the men agreed. 'Our cause is not noted for its wealthy supporters.'

They all laughed, then Saffron gasped in pain as Olivia grasped her wrist and ordered, 'Piero, you take the wheel. Guido, help me get the handcuffs on her.'

Guido was the smaller of the two men, the one Saffron disliked the most, and she flinched away from the sourness of his body as he bent towards her. Although not tall, he was well muscled, his fingers easily gripping both her wrists, and she was forced to submit to the final indignity of having her wrists constrained in the handcuffs attached to the side of the Land Rover.

'Just in case you try to do something foolish like jumping out,' Olivia warned her. 'Not that you would. You are not exactly the stuff of martyrs, are you? Does it never worry you that while you live off champagne and caviare, dressed in fine silks and satins, there are people in the world living from hand to mouth, forced always into giving a tithe of their pitiful income to support their oppressors? But soon all that will end. The curse that has held our people in bondage for so long will be removed.'

Her fanaticism terrified Saffron. She didn't begin to understand what the other girl was talking about, but an inner instinct urged her to show interest, as though by listening to her captors she might discover the key to her own freedom.

'You believe in Communism?' she hazarded.

'You are right.' Olivia's dark eyes glittered. 'Each man and woman has the right to be equal, but they are denied that basic human right; wealth which should be evenly spread among them is held by far too few, the Church especially, but soon all that will end.'

Saffron couldn't believe her ears. 'But Italy is a Catholic country,' she protested. 'The people would never abandon their religion.'

'Then we shall have to use force,' Guido cut in. 'In the end they will see the wisdom of what we are doing. The Church is rotten and corrupt; a money-making machine feeding off the people. We will take that wealth and share it among them.'

Surely they couldn't believe such a thing could be accomplished, Saffron thought, appalled, but she saw that they did. Each of them was wearing a rapt, fixed expression, zeal written clearly on their features. Did Nico share their fanatical views?

'The organisation has strong supporters in the universities,' Olivia told her. 'Our young people see how false the Christian religion is. "Blessed are the meek,"' she quoted scornfully. 'That is what they say, but saying and doing are two different things, and in this world the meek get trodden underfoot.'

'And you intend to change that?'

'It is what many people think we intend to do,' Piero told her mirthlessly. 'But there will always be those who hold power and those who yield before it, but before we can rebuild first we have to destroy, and for that we need money—money we raise by ransoming rich prizes such as you.'

'Of all the so-called terrorist organisations in the world, we are the most feared,' Olivia boasted. 'More so than the P.L.O. or the Red Brigade. Already we have been responsible for the deaths of over a thousand people.'

'But you're killing innocent people,' Saffron expostulated. 'Surely you would gain more support for your cause by using reasoned argument, not mindless terrorism?'

'The way rich dictators do?' Piero scoffed. 'We have discovered that one machine-gun speaks more potently that a million useless words, although the day will come when the world will listen to our words, even if we have to destroy everyone who tries to stand in our way.'

The venom in his voice terrified Saffron. To her their words were those of political extremists, the enormity of what they were suggesting almost impossible for her to grasp.

'Out!'

She had been so engrossed in her thoughts that she hadn't realised the Land Rover had stopped.

'Hurry!' Olivia ordered, almost pushing her out of the Land Rover as she unlocked the handcuffs. 'Don't keep Guido waiting,' she warned Saffron. 'He gets impatient, and when he gets impatient...'

She didn't finish the threat, but she didn't need to. Saffron could see the man grinning at her coarsely, as he lolled against the side of the Land Rover, picking his teeth.

'Why don't I just give her a sample of what's in store?' he suggested, moving towards her. His fingers had grasped her shirt front and Saffron had stiffened rigidly into her seat, before Olivia responded with an obvious ring of regret,

'Nico said not to touch her.'

Guido grimaced. 'Because he wants her for himself?' he suggested. 'And besides, how would he know? He won't be the first man she's had, by all accounts, and she's a hot little piece.'

'Nico doesn't want her,' Olivia denied heatedly, her eyes flashing venomously over Saffron's slender body. 'He despises her and all she stands for, you've heard him...

'Get out!' she ordered Saffron again, and Saffron did so shakily, the thought of Guido touching her making her almost physically sick, blotting out her mental anguish. Thank God they didn't know the truth, she thought half hysterically.

If they did ... She shuddered violently, realising that the destruction of her innocence would be merely amusing to a man like Guido.

The farmhouse was set among a few acres of scrubby olives and neglected vines, half a dozen painfully thin cows in a small paddock attached to the main building.

'Another idea of Nico's,' Olivia told her, watching her. 'If anyone comes up here poking around we're just another poor family trying to get a living out of a run-down smallholding. Guido and Piero are my brothers.'

'And Nico?' Saffron asked unwisely, wishing she hadn't when she saw the triumph glittering in the other girl's eyes, knew that she had wanted her to ask.

'Oh, Nico plays the same role as he does in real life,' she told Saffron softly. 'He is my man, my lover.' She laughed suddenly. 'You stupid, little rich fool! Did you honestly think a man such as Nico would want a woman like you? A woman who has no conception of anything apart from her clothes and her jewellery?' Her mouth twisted mockingly, and Saffron felt a sudden upsurge of reciprocal anger.

'At least that's better than those half-baked ideas you call your "cause",' she taunted, flinching as Olivia grasped a handful of her hair, twisting it until pain lanced through her scalp, her fingers leaving a scarlet imprint on Saffron's face when she hit her.

Saffron wanted to retch with nausea, caused more by the sudden display of violence than pain. Physical violence had always been something she had abhorred, and this was the woman Nico preferred to her; had they laughed about her together, planning her capture, planning how Nico would make love to her?

'It was his duty,' Olivia told her, reading her mind. 'Do not think he desired you—he hates you and your sort. If it wasn't for the money your father will pay to get you back he would kill you with no more regret that he would stamp on a snake.'

It was just beginning to dawn on Saffron that she was actually held prisoner by these political fanatics, whose respect for human life was nil, and Nico was one of them. Just for a moment she verged on the humiliation of completely breaking down, and then with almost superhuman effort managed to restrain herself. She must fix her thoughts of escaping and revenge; she must give herself something to work for.

All too soon she was inside the farmhouse. Downstairs there was merely one large, primitive room with a mud floor, baked hard over the years, and the most basic of kitchen arrangements in one corner, with a large woodburning range and a single tap. They had walked past a small building set on its own, and Saffron shuddered to think of the primitive sanitary arrangements. Would her captors try to indoctrinate her with their beliefs? If they tried she would strongly resist their attempts, but she suspected that their organisation did not make converts of its victims and that they saw her merely in terms of the money she would bring in, just as Nico had seen her. Nico! Why did she still have to feel this senseless pain whenever she thought of him? The man she had thought he was simply hadn't existed. He had been a daydream, a figure of romance and fiction conjured up by her own need.

'Come!'

The curt word and the painful tug on her arm which accompanied it jerked Saffron back to reality. Olivia indicated that she was to walk up the rickety wooden stairs leading to the upper storey. Four doors opened off the small landing and one of them bore a new, shiny padlock. Olivia opened it and pushed back the door, disturbing clouds of dust as she thrust Saffron inside. The room was small with a small window, the air stale. A narrow camp bed occupied one corner, a sleeping bag flung down beside it.

'Your room,' Olivia told her in a parody of politeness. 'I trust the *signorina* finds everything to her liking?'

The door was closed and locked before Saffron could make any comment.

Left to her own devices, she ran to the window, but she could see nothing other than the barren countryside and the narrow river meandering through one of the meadows. They were professionals, she acknowledged, mentally reviewing her situation; by the time her father learned that she was missing it would be far too late for anyone to find her. She had read about these politically motivated organisations; ruthless fanatics whose vicious treatment of their victims was not something she dared allow herself to dwell on, and yet unbidden, all the horror stories she had ever read came crowding into her mind. There had been the Getty heir; he had lost an ear, hadn't he; and then Patty Hearst, forced to join the 'gang' who had kidnapped her, and there were dozens of others. All at once the self-control which had sustained her from the beginning of her ordeal deserted her. Her whole body started to tremble, and she had to force back a desire to scream and scream until she was hoarse. Panic, once allowed to force its way through her guard, flooded her mind. She flung herself face down on the camp bed, muffling the sound of her crying with the sleeping bag as tears overwhelmed her. And then to compound her misery, hunger pangs gnawed insistently at her stomach. Were they planning to starve her in addition to everything else? Her tears stopped flowing, and as she straightened up she acknowledged that she had probably needed that brief release. Gradually her body stopped trembling. Footsteps on the stair alerted her. Frantically scrubbing at her face, she prayed that in the dimness of the badly lit room no one would be able to tell that she had been crying. Stiff with tension, she listened.

'Guido, come back!' she heard Olivia call. 'Nico's here!'

The footsteps faded away and Saffron breathed a sigh of relief. Something about Guido's small reptilian eyes made her skin crawl with revulsion. Dear God, if she ever managed to escape she would make them pay—all of them; but most of all Nico. Nico, who had tricked her into believing that he cared about her, when in reality all he cared about was her money!

'So, you understand the position?' They were standing in the downstairs room, Nico and Olivia ranged on one side of the bare, scrubbed table, Saffron on the other, while Guido and Piero stood guard.

It was barely dawn, but never had Saffron been so glad to see the end of a night. She hadn't slept. It had been impossible, and now she was down here in this ramshackle building, being told that her first wrong move would mean a bullet in her leg or worse.

"Why don't you simply keep me under lock and key?' she said tonelessly, ignoring the sudden glint of warning in Nico's eyes. How he had changed! How could she had ever thought of him as a kindred spirit? He was the hardest and most unfeeling man she had ever met.

'We are not so foolish,' he told her coolly. 'This place could be searched. If it is you will behave exactly as you have been told. You are Olivia's cousin—a little lacking in the wits, but useful about the house. We have just taken over the farmstead and are working hard to get it back in shape—and we will work,' he told the others, suddenly switching his attention from Saffron to the others. 'It will be excellent practice, comrades, for the days to come when all of us are equal and the world is a perfect Marxist state.'

If she hadn't known better Saffron could have sworn there was a certain element of mockery in his last words. Olivia immediately took exception to his comment. 'We shall never work the land like peasants, Nico,' she told him. 'That is not . . .'

'I thought the most important tenent of communism was that all must be equal; that there could be no élite,' Saffron interrupted.

Olivia spared her a withering glare. 'There must always be those who take control. Our organisation is already grooming men and women for these positions, but they will not be motivated by greed or the lust for power as present capitalist governments are. We will be there to guide the people for their own benefit . . .'

'The words of dictators the world over,' Saffron taunted.

'That is enough!' Nico rapped out. 'Now, as I was saying. If the police should come searching for you here, one false move and you and they will be killed . . .'

'So much bloodshed,' Saffron said bitterly. 'Can any cause be worth it?'

'Ask your capitalist government,' Olivia suggested. 'They have grown fat and lazy on the deaths of others. Ask them if it is not worth it.'

'You will find it a hard task trying to convert her, Olivia,' Nico interrupted. 'You forget her father is one of those capitalists.'

Saffron could have told him that her father had started his working life in a very humble capacity and had built up his present business empire solely through his own efforts, but she chose to say nothing. Dared she take the risk of exposing the gang to the police for what they were, were the former to search the farmstead? With reluctance she admitted that she did not. It wasn't just that she was risking her own life, she was risking theirs as well.

'Very wise,' Nico mocked hatefully, correctly interpreting the look in her eyes. 'And just remember it whenever you are feeling reckless. Guido and Piero have their orders and they will not hesitate to obey them. Oh, and one other thing. Olivia tells me that you have been trying to establish some sort of rapport with Guido. For your own sake I advise that you desist. Guido is completely loyal to the cause, and although he has a weakness for women you would be unwise in the extreme to think of using that weakness to make your escape. Guido is perfectly capable of making love to you with one breath and killing you with the next. You are a body to him, Saffron, not a person, and you would do well to remember that.'

'How could I forget it?' Saffron retorted bitterly. 'It's something you and he share in common. A teaching of your organisation, perhaps,' she suggested sarcastically, and had the satisfaction of seeing him pale slightly beneath his tan. So he did have vulnerable points after all. He hadn't liked being bracketed with Guido. So much for equality, she thought cynically.

What would she do if the police did come? Could she perhaps attract their attention? Or would they recognise her? Hope flared, and as though he saw it in her eyes and recognised the reason for it, Nico announced briefly, 'We'll have to do something about your appearance.' He eyed her for a moment and then said to Olivia, 'As soon as I've taken the photographs to send to her father, you can cut her hair.'

Her hair! Saffron's hands went protectively to it. She had always worn it long. It was like liquid silk, her father had told her just a few short weeks ago. Too late she saw the triumph in Olivia's eyes and knew how much she would relish her task.

Breakfast had been bread—a coarse brown bread—and goat's cheese, with mugs of strong coffee. Saffron had forced hers down, telling herself that she must keep her strength up. She would accomplish nothing by starving herself.

In order to take the photographs he planned to send to her father Nico made her sit in an upright wooden chair, while Olivia manacled her hands. The Italian girl wrenched Saffron's arms painfully behind her back, causing a small gasp of pain to escape her tightly closed lips. Nico's eyes narrowed as he witnessed the small cruelty. 'That's enough,

Olivia,' he warned. 'We don't want to get Daddy in a panic at the sight of his little girl in tears.'

'Why not?' Olivia objected. 'It will encourage him to pay the ransom that much sooner.'

'It could also panic him into doing something foolish,' Nico corrected coolly. 'Remember what happened with John Hunter.'

Saffron's heart thumped as she heard the name of her father's great friend.

'You were responsible for killing John Hunter?' she whispered painfully, her eyes fixed on Nico's face.

'Not personally,' he mocked smoothly.

'Nico doesn't care for bloodshed,' Piero intervened. 'He is too nice.'

'I am too sensible,' Nico corrected calmly. 'Murdering Hunter achieved nothing and in fact cost us money, as the ransom was never paid over. By all means let us dispose of the evidence.' His eyes rested coolly and without emotion on Saffron's strained face. 'But let us first of all make sure we have our money.'

If anything he was worse than the others, Saffron thought bitterly. They at least had the excuse of their belief in their cause, if excuse it could be called, but Nico, she sensed, did not share their commitment. He was too cynical, too aloof. So why had he allied himself to these people? What was he doing with them? She could only think of one reason—money, and her heart thudded erratically. Could she perhaps persuade him to set her free by offering a bribe, by suggesting that her father might pay him to return her to him unharmed?

'Smile,' he ordered in a softly persuasive voice, as he set up the camera. 'For Daddy.'

Firmly compressing her lips, Saffron refused even to look at the camera. With a faint sigh Nico approached her, gripping her chin firmly as he forced her head round.

'Why are you indulging her in this fashion?' Olivia demanded, eyes narrowing suspiciously. 'You are going soft, my friend.'

As though to refute her words, Nico's grip of Saffron's chin tightened painfully, his eyes grey chips of ice as he turned her round to face the camera.

'Smile, Saffron,' he told her emotionlessly, 'or else I might change my mind and agree with Olivia that tears would have more effect on your father.'

'How can you do this?' Saffron hissed at him, forgetting the mental vow she had made not to lower herself to his level by exchanging conversation with him.

'Very easily, when I am dealing with gullible fools like you,' Nico mocked softly, watching the colour drain from her face.

'You . . . you sadist!' she whispered sickly. 'I suppose your twisted mind thinks that's something to brag about—how you fooled and deceived me? and I fell for it. Well, go on,' she cried bitterly, 'tell them. I'm sure they'll all thoroughly approve. You aren't fit to be part of the human race!' she finished in a voice thick with tears.

'Be careful,' Nico warned tersely, 'otherwise I might find it necessary to prove to you how anti-social I can be.' His eyes rested meaningfully on the curves of her breasts, and to her chagrin Saffron felt herself colour, as she looked fully at him. It was what he wanted.

Flashbulbs popped around her as Nico moved, quickly snapping her before she could look away, and she was forced to admit that he had outwitted her. She hated him—hated him!

'And now the tape,' she came back to earth to hear Nico saying in a brisk businesslike fashion. 'Let's have a few words for dear old Daddy, telling him how much you're enjoying yourself.'

'Go to hell!' Saffron shot back at him as he produced a miniature recorder. 'I'm not saying a word!'

The way in which he advanced on her, surefooted as a mountain cat, coupled with his calm, 'Oh, but I think you are,' had the effect of completely undermining her willpower,

'We can do this two ways,' Nico continued evenly. 'Cleanly and without any mess or fuss, or . . .'

He paused expectantly, and Saffron knew that he wasn't making idle threats. For a moment she longed to reiterate her earlier comment, but common sense prevailed, and feeling her hatred of him grow by the second she forced back the defiant words, and managed a husky, 'What do I have to say?' trying to ignore her outraged pride that she should capitulate so easily beneath the threat of force, but the effect of her incarceration in her small prison, plus the awful inescapability of her capture, had seriously undermined her spirit.

The tape recording was mercifully brief, simply half a dozen sentences telling her father that she was in great danger; that he was not to go to the police and that he must do everything the kidnappers wanted.

'Excellent,' Nico mocked when she had finished. 'See how easy life can be when you co-operate?'

This time she did give in to her emotions, her muttered, 'God, I hate you!' bringing only narrowed grey eyes in a concentrated gaze on her face, for a few telling seconds before she flushed, her eyes unable to hold that inimical gaze.

'Right,' Nico announced when he had packed the small tape away safely, 'everyone to their posts. Saffron, you will help Olivia with the lunch. What?' he murmured silkily when she started to protest that they might have kidnapped her but they couldn't force her into behaving like a household drudge. 'You find housework too menial? Perhaps you would prefer to work on the vines with Guido.'

How she loathed him! He had found her weakest spot with diabolical ease. He had known how she felt about Guido, how he made her flesh crawl with sick horror.

Shaking her head numbly, she followed Olivia towards the crude sink, Nico's mocking laughter ringing in her ears.

Olivia was obviously not particularly domesticated, and with a grimace she pushed the bowl of vegetables towards Saffron.

'Here, you do them,' she commanded brusquely, subjecting Saffron to a lecture on their organisation's view of the future role of women, which Saffron gathered did not include such mundane chores as preparing vegetables for a stew. And to think she had always thought her exclusive finishing school had left her ill-equipped for real life! Compared with the 'school' Olivia had finished in her experience was vast. Who did Olivia and her like think was going to provide the basic requirements such as food, clothing, all the little home comforts the recipients took for granted, in the brave new world Olivia and her like were determined to create?

As she scraped carrots methodically, Saffron glanced down at the knife she was holding. Small and sharp . . . Could she, dared she pocket it?

She glanced over her shoulder. Guido was standing by the door cleaning his gun. Piero had gone outside, and Olivia was talking in a low voice to Nico. Her heart started thumping heavily as she curled her fingers round the knife.

'Finished?'

Olivia snatched the cast-iron saucepan away, and Saffron quickly slipped the knife into the pocket of her jeans, the blood pounding in her ears. With every painfully constricted breath she expected to hear one of them commanding her harshly to stop where she was, but unbelievably no one did.

'When am I to cut her hair?' Olivia questioned Nico. 'We cannot take the risk of leaving her like this.'

Nico looked at her and Saffron's pulse quickened nervously. Had he guessed about the knife? There was a curious expression in his eyes as they rested briefly on the silky fall of her hair, and for a moment Saffron almost thought she heard curt regret in his brusque, 'No!'

'Very well, then,' he agreed. 'Take her upstairs.'

Guido was leaning against the stairs, and Saffron was forced to brush past him. He grinned wolfishly, his eyes on her breasts, and she recoiled.

'Look at her!' Olivia sneered to Nico. 'The shrinking society virgin, I don't think. Why so nice?' she demanded of Saffron. 'Guido is no different from any of the other men you have lain with. He has had many rich lovers. Wealthy women like a man who has machismo; who is a little rough with them, don't they, *caro*? Or is it for

Nico's benefit that you appear so pale and afraid?' she asked viciously, her eyes narrowing suspiciously.

'Be careful, *amico*,' she warned Nico softly. 'She will try and get round you—I know her sort.'

Upstairs in her narrow prison, Olivia pushed her down into the room's single chair. Despite her lack of inches the Italian girl was strong, and Saffron flinched beneath the pressure of her fingers, trying not to wince as Olivia tugged brutally at her hair, hacking at the long dark auburn strands with a rough pair of kitchen scissors.

She would not cry, she told herself; she would not, and yet it was impossible not to feel anguish as she saw her hair falling to the floor at her feet.

'Not quite your usual style,' Olivia jeered when she had finished. 'I read that in Northern Ireland they have a custom of tarring and feathering female traitors. I believe the only way to remove the tar is to shave off all their hair, is this so?'

'Why do you ask?' Saffron was proud of the steadiness of her voice. 'Are you thinking that perhaps your organisation could adopt the custom for female traitors?'

'My guess is that your father would pay up much quicker if the photographs we sent him showed you tarred and feathered in such a fashion. I shall speak to Nico.'

It was too much for Saffron. Somehow the hidden knife was in her hand, her hand raised towards Olivia. She heard the other girl's furious protest, heard her cry out for Nico, heard him command Guido to remain on guard as he came rushing up the wooden stairs and into the room, taking in the scene at a glance.

'Saffron! Give me the knife!'

He moved behind her, grasping her wrist firmly, but surprisingly not painfully, forcing it back, and uncurling her fingers so that the knife fell to the floor, Olivia's stream of invective washing over her as the Italian girl grasped what was left of her hair and tugged viciously, slapping Saffron's face.

'Olivia, stop it!' Nico ordered.

'Look what she has done to me!' Olivia protested, releasing Saffron to show Nico the small scratch on her arm. 'I will make her pay for this!' She reached for the scissors.

Smooth as silk Nico moved, restraining Olivia in much the same way as he had restrained Saffron only seconds before,

'Have you searched her?' he demanded quietly.

'She's not touching me again!'

The words were out before Saffron could stop them, recognition coming too late as she saw the expression flaring smokily in the dark grey eyes before Nico said softly, 'Very well then, I shall search you.'

'No!'

Her explosive protest brought a mirthless laugh from Olivia. 'Leave the scissors with me,' Nico instructed Olivia, 'then go downstairs and help Guido keep a look out.'

Saffron could sense that the Italian girl was reluctant to leave them alone, but it was equally obvious that she dared not ignore Nico.

For several seconds after she had gone Nico didn't move, simply saying coolly, 'Now come here. Let's get it over with.'

'You're not touching me!'

This time there was less conviction in her voice and she started to back into the corner of the room, even though Nico hadn't moved.

And then he did—so swiftly that she was pinioned in his arms before she could move, his breath clean and cool against her forehead muscles taut under the faded bush shirt he was wearing, crumpled but clean, and she found herself wondering irrelevantly how he alone of all of them managed to look so clean and groomed at the same time as she croaked pleadingly, her hand protectively warding him off, 'No!'

CHAPTER FOUR

'I INTEND to search you, not rape you.'

The cool matter-of-fact tone added anger to her cringing disbelief.

'Why not combine the two?' she threw at him bitterly. 'Isn't that the way men like you normally get their kicks?'

'Men like me?' His tone was so soft she could almost have believed she imagined the rage suppressed in it, but a muscle was beating erratically in his jaw, a white line of anger tautening his mouth. 'Are you sure you're not the one who's looking for kicks?' he demanded smoothly. 'Spoiled little rich girls like you have a reputation for ... Oh no, you don't!' He grasped her wrist as Saffron lifted her hand, hard fingers closing round it, forcing it down and then pulling her ruthlessly towards him.

His clinical exploration of her body was the most humiliating experience she had ever undergone, the look in his eyes grimly explicit as he withdrew his hands.

'See?' he drawled mockingly. 'Hardly a picture of uncontrolled lust, am I?'

'You're ... you're ... despicable!' Saffron spat at him, hating him. 'And I hate you!'

She was frighteningly close to tears and had to turn away from him so that he couldn't tell.

'Saffron?'

Was it her imagination, or had his voice softened slightly? She turned hesitantly and awkwardly, and stumbled. Nico's hand shot out to steady her, his fingers accidentally brushing the tips of her breasts. A sensation not unlike a tiny electric shock shivered through her, widening her eyes and causing her pulses to race with sensual excitement.

'I'm all right. I . . . I want you to go,' she had been about to say, but as she looked away she became aware of the burgeoning hardness of her nipples clearly outlined against the taut pull of her tee-shirt.

Hot, guilty colour flooded her face.

'Get out of here!' she snapped. 'And don't touch me! I can't stand you touching me . . .'

It was the wrong thing to say. His eyes were sardonically derisive. 'No?' he drawled, his glance resting thoughtfully on her breasts. 'I'd say you've got your wires crossed somewhere, Saffron,' he added unforgivably, 'and that what you'd really like is for me to touch you one hell of a lot.'

'No!'

'No?' He smiled dulcetly. 'Let's just put that to the test, shall we?'

She was in his arms before she could move, his mouth moving exploratively against her own. She kept her lips tightly closed, trying to pretend that it was Guido who held her, trying to force her body to feel revulsion and not pleasure as Nico's hands swept upwards under her rib-cage, his lean fingers possessing the swollen heat of her breasts beneath her tee-shirt. Her gasp of dismay as he used one hand to release the catch of her bra gave him the purchase he was seeking. His mouth investigated the moist sweetness of hers, subjecting her to an intimacy never previously experienced.

While her lips softened and clung without her

sanction his fingers possessed and aroused the throbbing fullness of her breasts. She was clamped against his body, the hardness of male muscles imprinted against her softness, and yet it wasn't enough. A tiny, rebellious corner of her ignored all her exhortations to resist and reject and murmured instead how much it wanted to the pleasure of naked skin against skin.

With an aching cry, Saffron tore her mouth from Nico's, her eyes wide and bitter.

'Nico?'

Nico gave her a grim smile as Olivia called him. The expression in his eyes as he stepped away from her and towards the door made Saffron writhe in a torment of self-disgust. What had possessed her? How could she have responded to such clinical lovemaking? She hated Nico! And yet her body had undeniably responded to him. Why?

Only when she was quite sure she was alone did she give way to tears, crying silently into open, upturned palms, her body shaking spasmodically. All around her lay swathes of dark, silky auburn hair, but it wasn't the loss of her smooth, sleek curtain of hair that she grieved for, but something deeper and less easy to understand. For a moment as Nico touched her something had come vitally alive inside her, and he had known it. There had been a second before she struggled when he had looked at her and she had known that somehow he had sensed her body's desire to respond against all logic and pride to the male command of his hand.

Her bag was in the room with her and she fished inside it for a pack of tissues. If only she had thought to put just one extra tee-shirt in it. With her tears drying on her skin she became aware of feeling hot and grubby. Her legs were dusty, but

there was no water in her room for her to wash.
Apart from Nico her captors didn't seem too
concerned with the niceties of civilisation and
personal cleanliness, not even Olivia, but Saffron
was fastidious about her person, and the fact that
she had not been able to bathe or even clean her
teeth filled her with distaste.

There was a river in the valley and she could see
it from her window. Just the sight of the gently
flowing water increased her longing to feel its cool
silkiness against her skin, and she wondered if she
dared ask for a bowl to wash in. Olivia would
probably delight in refusing her request and she
refused to ask any of the men. Guido, because
something about the way he watched her
frightened her, and Nico because she didn't want
him thinking that her interest in her personal
appearance had anything to do with him!

As the day wore on the inertia which enveloped
her—left on her own with nothing to do; nothing
to occupy either her hands or her mind except
the danger of her situation—deepened into a
thick grey miasma of misery, a nadir of
depression from which there was no merciful
escape into acceptance, just a constant mental
war against the admission that her life might
very well come to an end, here in this dusty grey
farmhouse.

During the afternoon she heard sounds of
movement down below her, but no one approached
her prison; she could see Guido working on the
vines and prayed for the police to arrive as Nico
had warned that they might.

If they did nothing was going to stop her from
trying to tell them who she was even if she was
shot down at least she would have tried—and

possibly caused their deaths as well? Saffron knew she couldn't do it.

She had seen Nico drive away shortly after he left her and he returned just as dusk was falling. He had been to send the tape and photographs to her father and Saffron tried to work out how long it would be before they heard from him. Obviously they wouldn't have sent them direct—that would make the farmhouse far too easy to trace. So what had Nico done? Sent them to Rome perhaps for onward transmission? It was immaterial really.

Olivia came and unlocked her prison door half an hour after Nico's return.

Appetising smells wafted upstairs as Saffron followed Olivia down, and she realised with a small start of surprise that she was actually hungry.

'Nico bought pasta and sauce to heat up,' Olivia explained when Piero raised his eyebrows and commented that something smelled good.

Saffron noticed how both Guido and Piero sat down to their meal without bothering to wash the earth from their hands, but Nico, who had changed into fresh snug-fitting and faded jeans and a soft white shirt, unbuttoned casually at the throat, rinsed his hands beneath the tap before joining them, even though he hadn't been working outside.

Saffron followed his example without asking permission, closing her eyes in sheer pleasure as the ice-cold water ran over her hot wrists.

'Fastidious, aren't we?' Olivia sneered. 'Hoping to impress Nico with our ladylike ways, is that it?'

'Some of us prefer to be clean and fresh.' Saffron responded woodenly, goaded by the other girl's open contempt.

'Meaning what exactly?' The dark eyes flashed

dangerously and as Olivia called, 'Nico, prisoner, or not, I'm not going to be insulted by this little bitch; either you tell her to watch her manners or I'll make sure she does,' Saffron knew that Olivia had deliberately goaded her, but why? So that she would have an opportunity to subject her to more physical punishment? Saffron had noticed already that none of the others dared to flout Nico's commands, and yet in many ways he seemed a little aloof and distant from them; even from Olivia, who was presumably his mistress.

The food had been surprisingly good, the pasta rich and moist, and Saffron was amazed at the speed with which she emptied her plate. Her mind might be in despair but her body still wanted feeding.

It was Nico who escorted her to her 'room' later in the evening. Once inside Saffron waited to hear the closing of the door and the key turning in the lock, but to her surprise he lingered.

'I could arrange for Olivia to take you down to the river so that you can bathe if you wish?' he suggested, almost hesitantly, or so it seemed, and for some reason what Saffron interpreted as pity in the look he gave her drove her to say bitterly, 'What's the matter? Do I offend your sensibilities in my grubby clothes? My body unwashed? Too bad! You'll just have to learn to live with it.'

Immediately the words were uttered she was regretting them, wishing she had accepted his offer, but it was too late to recall her rash statement now, for Nico was already turning back to the door, shrugging carelessly as he did so. 'Have it your own way,' he told her. 'I merely thought you might appreciate the opportunity to ... refresh yourself. From tomorrow evening one of us will walk with you—you must have exercise, and if you don't go willingly you will be forced.'

'Such concern for my well-being!' Saffron marvelled sardonically. 'Why? Don't you think I know how little chance I have of getting out of here alive?'

Unconsciously her voice was full of anguished pain, reflected in her eyes as she looked at him.

For a moment it almost seemed as though he understood and wanted to comfort her, but it must only have been a trick of the light, because he moved and once again his eyes were as cold and hard as they had always been, his voice soft as he asked, 'And if you don't, what would you miss the most? The arms of your latest lover: The feeling of expensive silk against your body? The glitter of jewels?'

'None of those things,' Saffron retorted huskily. 'What I would miss most would be the opportunity to breathe clean, fresh air, untainted by animals like you—Animals.' She laughed shrilly, the sound edged with hysteria. 'Animals don't do things like this to one another. They don't destroy and maim purely for financial gain, without a thought for the misery they're causing. How much have you asked my father for?'

'One million pounds,' Nico told her blandly. 'A nice round sum, don't you think?'

'You planned this right from the start—at the ball in Rome, didn't you?'

'Yes.' The admission was firm, refusing to betray regret or compassion.

'And knowing what was intended you were still able to ... to ...'

'Flirt with you?' he offered cynically. 'It was necessary, and not hard.' A muscle moved faintly in his jaw, lean and tanned and showing a slight shadow where he shaved. 'You're a very attractive woman, as I'm sure you already know, and the mood was right. What right-minded Italian male would have done otherwise?'

'Fool, fool!' her mind screamed at her. She had believed it meant something. She had behaved like a love-crazed teenager.

'You're a machine, not a man!'

For a moment she thought he was going to strike her again, but instead a look of grim comprehension darkened his eyes.

'You hate yourself because inadvertently you responded to me as a woman,' he stated calmly, his words bringing a surge of colour to her face. 'Do not. It was a perfectly normal reaction in the circumstances; a woman of your experience is bound to be responsive to a man, especially one who has already . . .'

'Tried to seduce her?' Saffron supplied for him.

He shrugged, his mouth hard.

'That implies an innocence which we both know you do not possess. Things will be much easier for you if you do not fight against them. I have no wish to hurt or humiliate you . . .'

Her bitter laugh silenced him.

'Look . . .' He reached for her, grasping her arms, and she flinched in his grasp.

'What are you trying to do?' she demanded angrily. 'Make Olivia jealous? Why don't you call her up here so that she can see . . .'

'You are determined to annoy me, aren't you? Or is this what you really want?'

Swift as a panther, his grasp tightened, drawing her against the hard male outline of his body, his hands moving from her shoulders to her back, moulding her against him, one hand circling the back of her neck, forcing it to bend, the other securing her against him.

'No!'

Her moaned protest was smothered beneath the fierce pressure of his mouth, and only when it possessed hers did Saffron realise how much she had infuriated him. He was obviously a man who was not used to being criticised by a woman, she thought hazily, trying to fight against the melting lethargy spreading through her body. His first touch had ignited fires she was finding it hard to control, every pulse in her body responding wildly to the heated pressure of his mouth. She could taste salt blood in her mouth from the bruising pressure of his lips, and instantly the pressure of his kiss relaxed, and his tongue touched her skin tasting her blood. A wave of pleasure, so fierce that it frightened her, left her weak and shaken, unable to understand what was happening to her. She hated him—loathed him!

'What are you trying to do?' she asked when at last he had released her.

His grim, 'I could ask you the same question,' silenced her for several seconds. On legs which threatened to buckle beneath her she walked to the window and stared out of it. Why did she experience this overwhelming sexual magnetism whenever Nico came within close range. She hated and detested the man, but her body seemed to crave him.

'If you feel like experimenting again, make sure you don't choose Guido,' Nico warned her, breaking the silence. 'You might get a response you didn't bargain for, unless Olivia's right and the thought of being mauled about excites you? Is that it?' he asked pointedly, his eyes on the shallow rise and fall of her breasts. 'Is that what you were hoping for? You've been watching too many movies,' he told her harshly. 'Desirable you might be, but not desirable enough for me to want to take you here and now.' His mouth twisted a little. 'When I make love I prefer comfort, clean sheets and a sweet-smelling woman in my arms.'

The gibe drove the colour from Saffron's face. 'Is that why you do things like this?' she demanded fiercely. 'So that you can afford to live in style? If that's the case why don't we come to some mutually beneficial arrangement?' An idea had just occurred to her, and before she lost her courage she was going to try and put it to the test. Swallowing the fear building up inside her, she leaned forward slightly, lips parted, fingers curling into the open collar of Nick's shirt.

'A million pounds could go a long way if you had it all to yourself.'

'What are you suggesting?' He didn't move, his eyes giving nothing away. He was like granite, Saffron thought wildly, unyielding, remorselessly crushing anything that got in his way.

'A double-cross?'

She shrugged, trying to appear calm and in control. 'Why not? Or are you going to tell me there's honour among thieves?' She said it sweetly enough, but the arrow found its mark. Her fingers were ruthlessly removed from his shirt, his expression distant as he looked down at her.

'And if I agreed? If I wanted more than a million pounds, if I wanted you, for instance?'

A hard lump seemed to have settled in her chest, causing a tight unremitting pain.

'I ... We might be able to come to some arrangement,' she managed breathlessly.

The look in his eyes frightened her and she
reached for him automatically, only to find he had
put the width of the room between them, his
mouth curling disdainfully as he studied her.

'Well, you're all the same, aren't you?' he
breathed at last, and Saffron could see his chest
rising and falling beneath the thin white shirt as
though he had been running. Awareness of the
deep undercurrent of anger possessing him ran
through her on a shock wave, although she didn't
know what she had done to cause it.

'Who the hell do you think you're deceiving?' he
said scornfully. 'Making with the big sacrifice.
Some sacrifice! You want me,' he told her flatly,
'and I wouldn't touch you now if you were the last
woman left on earth. Don't you think I know what
turns you on? Don't you think I know all about
the type of thrill women like you get from the
thought of being taken by force? If that's what you
want Guido is your man, not me—I like my sex
straight,' he told her brutally.

He was gone before she could retaliate, leaving
her feeling bruised and humiliated by his rejection,
and unable to understand what had happened.
One moment she had actually thought that she
might be able to use the bait of all the ransom
money as a means of dividing her captors; and
the next he had turned the tables on her implying
that she had been trying to persuade him to make
love to her when in reality she had been nerving
herself . . .

For what? an inner voice asked. She didn't want
him, Saffron defended bitterly. She hated him,
loathed him!

Saffron had been a prisoner for four days. The

hope she had nursed so hard at first had waned leaving in its place dull apathy. The days formed themselves into a set routine. In the morning her room was unlocked by Olivia, who brought up water for her to wash in and then escorted her to the primitive little hut set discreetly away from the farmhouse. Initially fastidious embarrassment had overwhelmed Saffron each time she was forced to endure this indignity, but her imprisonment and the very basic diet she was getting had worn away her resistance.

Every night before going to sleep she washed out the clothes she had worn during the day, but although they dried well enough overnight they were now beginning to look shabby. She felt ill-kempt and scruffy, but her personal appearance had taken a back seat to her fears for her safety.

In the evening they all ate a meal together in the room downstairs, often prepared by Saffron herself under the watchful eyes of her guards. Today Nico had been missing and she had been acutely aware of his absence, even though she had not spoken a single word to him since the day he had searched her. At first her determined avoidance of him had made Olivia laugh, but now Saffron often found the other girl watching her as though she found it hard to understand how she could be so indifferent to him.

But she wasn't indifferent. With nothing to do but brood on her situation Saffron found her hatred of him growing, feeding off her and draining her of the ability to think of anything else.

He had arrived while she had been checking the vines with Guido; a back-breaking task, and one from which she would gladly have stretched her aching back if she hadn't been sure that Nico would have taken the gesture as a sign of defeat. Somehow the two of them had become involved in a silent tussle of wills; Saffron knew her silence angered Nico, she had seen it in his eyes, and the knowledge had brought her perverse pleasure. He wanted to break her will, she was convinced of it; he wanted to reduce her to the kind of fear he no doubt expected from his victims. Well, she wasn't going to join their ranks!

'What's the matter? Too soft for honest-to-goodness work?' Guido jeered as she paused without stretching, his eyes lingering lasciviously on the rounded outline of her breasts.

The other three members of the gang were constantly taunting her, but Saffron had quickly learned to shut herself off from their gibes, although a deep inborn instinct warned her to be wary with Guido. Olivia seemed to deliberately throw the two of them together, and pride alone prevented Saffron from correcting her when she implied to Nico that Saffron had spent most of the day with her.

In many ways she would have preferred to remain shut up in her prison, but Nico insisted that she spend the day outside in the fresh air, exercising her limbs. She couldn't understand why, Saffron reflected cynically. She was convinced now that she would never leave the farmhouse alive. Every day Nico had driven into town waiting for news from her father. They had given him a week to raise the ransom, and five days of that week were already gone. Saffron had tried on several occasions to imagine her father's state of mind, the anxiety he must be going through, his frantic attempts to raise the cash, but her world had become bounded by her guards, speculation about what was happening outside her prison too painful to be endured for very long.

Olivia had killed one of the scraggy chickens that scratched around the farmhouse and Saffron had casseroled it as best she could. It smelled quite appetising when she and Guido walked into the farmhouse. Nico was sitting down reading a newspaper, Olivia beside him, arms twined round him. He looked up and Saffron looked away immediately, her mouth tightening.

'Your father at least shows some sense,' Nico commented. 'There is nothing in the papers about your disappearance, merely a small item in one of the London gossip columns to the effect that you are holidaying with friends.'

His smile mocked and infuriated her, but Saffron refused to respond. She started to walk towards the stairs and had almost reached them when he stretched out a hand and grasped her wrist. Saffron tensed, her glance drawn unwilling to meet his, their eyes clashing. Beneath the thin cotton shirt he was wearing she could see the dark crispness of his body hair. Something stirred inside her, alien and unwanted, and she pulled tensely away, desperate to escape the proximity of his body.

'Where are you going?'

'To my room.'

How childish it sounded; petulant and sulky, almost.

'Why?'

His voice was cool, the word silky, but an atavistic apprehension shuddered down her spine.

'Because I want to be alone,' she retorted flippantly. 'Any objections?'

'Let her go, Nico,' Olivia urged. 'She cannot escape, and wouldn't try.' Her mouth curled contemptuously. 'She is too soft to know how to. All her life she has used her father's money and name to open doors for her; so much so that she is incapable now of opening them for herself.'

That's not true! The words formed in her mind but were never spoken. Pride kept her silent, and honesty compelled her to admit that a year ago Olivia could have had good grounds for flinging the accusations at her.

'Nico!'

Piero's anxious undertone call from outside brought Olivia and Guido out of their chairs, and Nico released Saffron's arm as he hurried to the door.

Saffron caught the word 'police' and her heart leapt with hope. Could they be looking for her? Had Maria reported her absence and had the police realised what might have happened to her? If only she could attract their attention in some way!

Tension filled the shabby farmhouse as the police vehicle bumped along the narrow track. The guns normally so much in evidence were put out of sight, only Guido playing warningly with the knife he always carried. Her mouth dry, Saffron heard the vehicle stop and then the sound of voices.

The door was thrust open and two men in uniform strode in, their eyes inspecting the shabby room.

'You have not been here very long?' one of them questioned, Nico who was lounging casually in front of her, but between her and the police, Olivia had slipped upstairs, and Nico had warned Saffron that were she to attempt to escape both she and the police would be shot down as they left. Saffron knew he was not exaggerating, but she couldn't let the opportunity pass without some attempt to alert the police.

'I inherited the farm from my uncle,' Nico explained. 'It is run down, but we hope to set it to rights.'

'You are not from round these parts?'

Again Nico shrugged. 'From Rome,' he told them, 'but I prefer the country to the city, as do my brothers.'

The man's eyes were on Saffron as his companion drifted round the room.

'Your sister?' he questioned Nico.

Blessing the fact that she could understand and speak Italian, Saffron interjected quickly, 'No, I . . .'

'She is my wife,' Nico answered quickly, moving backwards, his arm coming round Saffron's tense shoulders in apparent affection. Only she was aware of the biting grasp of the fingers bruising her flesh and the warning flare in the smoke-grey eyes.

'Will you stay and eat with us?'

Refusing, the two men headed towards the door. Saffron moved frantically in the constricting circle of Nico's arm, praying that one of them would turn and see her distress, but although one of them hesitated, neither of them turned. Guido walked to their vehicle with them and as she listened to the fading voices a terrible enervating sickness filled her. Her final hope was gone, and total lethargic depression possessed her.

Nico released her just as Olivia appeared from upstairs, her eyes moving suspiciously over them. Olivia was jealous, Saffron saw wearily, but she lacked the energy to make any use of the discovery. She was going to die. The knowledge filled and obsessed her. No matter what her father did he would not be able to save her. She shuddered and felt rather than saw Nico frown. Why was he pretending to feel concern for her? All of them knew that she was simply a commodity, a means of raising money for their cause. She fingered the still tender flesh of her face where he had struck her, feeding her hatred.

Saffron had no appetite for the chicken casserole. She had eaten very little for breakfast either, and had to choke back bitter laughter when Nico ordered her to finish her meal.

'Why?' she demanded. 'You're going to kill me anyway, so I might as well do the job for you.'

Olivia laughed. 'She is not as stupid as I thought. Or perhaps she is trying to cultivate your pity, *caro*. She has read too many newspaper stories about the relationships that develop in these situations between captor and prey.'

'You have to eat,' Nico told her unemotionally, ignoring Olivia. 'Has she been getting plenty of exercise?' he demanded of Guido.

The other man shrugged. 'She has been working in the fields this afternoon.'

'And every night one of us walks with her as you instructed,' Olivia told him.

'You will eat, or I will feed you myself,' Nico told Saffron.

'Have you heard anything from London?' Olivia interrupted him. 'Was there . . .'

'So far her father has followed our instructions to the letter.' Nico told her. 'He is trying to raise the money and hopes to have it within the stipulated time.'

'He'd better—otherwise we shall be sending his daughter back to him piecemeal.' Olivia's dark eyes glittered at the prospect, and this time when Saffron pushed her plate away untouched Nico made no attempt to chastise her.

'The sooner it's over the better,' Guido opined. 'I'm sick of this place. Give me Rome any day!'

It had gone dark outside while they were eating and in the velvet softness of the night the crickets chirruped ceaselessly, tiny moths hurling themselves at the windows as they sought the light.

'Come,' Nico instructed Saffron when they had finished eating. 'Tonight I will walk with you.'

She wanted to refuse; she could feel Olivia's eyes boring into her back like twin knives and had seen the flash of resentment in the glance Guido gave him, but Olivia had developed a habit of slipping silently away when she was supposed to be walking with her, leaving her alone with Guido, whose eyes roamed too hotly over her body.

There was a heavy stillness in the air which brought a fine film of perspiration to her skin the minute they stepped outside. She would give anything for a shower, Saffron thought longingly, quelling a sudden stupid urge to laugh as she recalled macabre jokes she had often been amused by, concerning a prisoner's last wishes. It seemed a lifetime ago since she had laughed naturally; she was beginning to understand how religious cults worked on their converts; shut away from the rest of the world, at the complete mercy of strangers, it was dangerously easy to feel one's judgment slipping away and one's willpower disintegrating.

Nico steered her in the direction of the river, almost as though he had read her mind and wanted to deliberately add to her torture. The warm male scent of his body reached her through the scents of the countryside around them, her senses so attuned to him that it frightened her.

Nico's offer that she could bathe in the river had never been repeated, and pride had prevented Saffron from asking, just as she refused to ask Nico for anything, no matter how acute her physical discomfort.

'You know, you're different from what I expected.'

The quiet comment caught her off guard, and she almost missed her footing as she stopped in the darkness to look up at him, searching his face for signs of mockery, but there were none.

'In what way?'

Somehow the cloak of darkness made it easier to talk, to put her hatred away from her, how ever temporarily.

She felt him shrug beside her.

'In every way—more vulnerable, and yet tougher, more resilient.'

Saffron tensed, suspecting a trap, her voice faintly brittle as she said bitterly, 'Not quite the rich bitch you expected? Not just a spoiled Daddy's girl who thinks she can buy her way out of anything? I'm not stupid. I know the statistics; I know why I'm here, and if you expect me to get down on my knees and beg for my life when I know that you're going to kill me.'

'And if you didn't know?'

'Is that what you want? For me to crawl and cry? Why? does it turn you on? Make a change from Olivia's masculinity?' she asked cuttingly. 'I've never begged any man for anything and I'm not going to start now!'

'No?'

Nico turned towards her and in the moonlight Saffron saw the cynicism ingrained into the hard planes of his face. 'That isn't how I heard it,' he said softly. 'Word is that that you're one of the easiest lays around—and the best. A real tough little lady who knows how to get her man when she wants him.'

'But I don't want you!' The husky denial was raw with an emotion Saffron wasn't going to try to name. Just listening to Nico speak had left her as bruised and aching as though she had been beaten. She knew about her reputation, of course; and sickness swept over her as she remembered her initial foolish belief that something special existed between them. Her fingers curled into her palms, her nails now devoid of varnish, and broken from the work she had been forced to endure.

'Even raving nymphomanics don't necessarily want every man they set eyes on,' she threw at him bitterly. 'What do you do when you aren't doing this for a living? Hire yourself out to middle-aged millionairesses?'

She gasped when his hands grasped her body beneath her armpits, threshing wildly as she tried to kick his shins. One brief glance at the icy fury of his expression told her that she had gone too far. Far enough for him to kill her now? she wondered. All at once she wanted to beg him not to torture her any more, to make her death swift and painless. Her eyes darkened with the burden of her emotions, the ragged urchin cut Olivia had given her unintentionally emphasising the delicacy of her bone structure and the fragility of her body, almost too thin after the weight loss of the last few days.

'Saffron . . .'

She veiled her eyes immediately, hating the tinge of compassion in his voice, rejecting the pity she could sense in him.

'What's the matter?' she jeered. 'Having second thoughts? Why don't you mention them to Olivia? I'm sure she'll have no problem in disposing of me when the time comes. She'll enjoy it.'

Only bitter anger had prompted the words, but Saffron sensed by the tenseness of his body that Nico was reacting to them.

'Perhaps she will,' he agreed smoothly. 'And if you're trying to goad me into losing my self-control . . .' He muttered something under his breath as the moonlight revealed the contempt in her eyes and then she was in his arms, feeling the heat coming off his body in the subtropical evening, his lips tracing the exposed line of her throat, his hands moulding her body against him.

Saffron tried to fight him, but his strength was too great. Fear leapt inside her when she felt Nico's hands on the bare skin of her back, stroking the supple contours of her spine, but it was a fear that soon gave way to spiralling tremors of pleasure.

Her lips parted in mute invitation without her being aware of it, her gasp of shock when Nico's hands moved round to cup her breasts lost in the warmth of his mouth on hers.

She forgot what had led up to this encounter; what had happened between them already and the reason she was here with him at all, as some deep primaeval instinct rose up to subdue everything but the need he was skilfully arousing within her. She had expected violence, but this was something else, and she had no power to withstand his subtle arousal of her untutored body.

When her bra was pushed aside to allow his seeking fingers access to the rounded warmth of her breasts, she was beyond caring that he was taking without permission the intimacy she had never allowed anyone else. When her breasts swelled and hardened to his touch she trembled with shock.

She shivered when one hand left her skin to slide possessively down to her hip, holding her so intimately against his own body that she was immediately aware of his arousal. Her flesh seemed to burn from the contact. She wanted to push him away, but instead her body seemed to cling erotically to his her arms lifting to encircle his shoulders, her breasts pressed against the hard warmth of his chest. She felt him tugging at her blouse, but didn't realise what he was doing until she felt the rough scrape of his body hair against the softness of her flesh, the contact instantly arousing. A strange sensation curled through the pit of her stomach, a husky moan torn from her throat as Nico's thumb stroked sensuously over the throbbing tip of her breast.

The male lips which had been exploring the soft vulnerability of her throat ceased their slow torment and the dark head bent. Tense excitement churned through her, desire flaring moltenly inside her as her fingers curled feverishly into his thick dark hair.

'Nico!'

His reactions were swifter than hers, and he had released her and stepped away before Olivia reached them, but Saffron didn't think for one moment that the Italian girl was deceived.

'We were concerned about you,' Olivia told him, 'you have been gone for so long.'

'Concerned?' Nico drawled coolly, 'or curious?'

'You have been making love to her!' Olivia blazed furiously, suddenly abandoning restraint. 'You have been making love to the little whore!'

'It is not a crime. Indeed one might almost call it one of the perks of the job. Surely you are not jealous, *cara*?'

He was deliberately baiting the other girl, Saffron realised, although she could not understand why, any more than she could understand what had driven him to touch her in the way that he had.

Her flesh still burned in memory of that touch, and no matter how much she berated herself now, she could not deny that she had responded to him. Her response had been purely physical, she assured herself; in her situation who would not act in a way that was out of character? But why had she experienced desire for Nico when all the other men she knew left her cold? It was just that she was in a highly charged emotional state, and those emotions had betrayed her.

Engrossed in her thoughts, she hadn't been aware of the fury in Olivia's eyes, but she was made abruptly conscious of the other girl's feelings on the way back to the farmhouse, when Olivia pushed her deliberately out of the way, almost causing her to stumble in the darkness. She had made a dangerous enemy in Olivia, Saffron acknowledged later when she had been locked in her room for the night, and the look she had given Saffron as they entered the farmhouse earlier had promised punishment for daring to usurp her own position with Nico.

Olivia was welcome to him, Saffron decided

wearily. Oh, she herself had been attracted to him initially, but that attraction hadn't lasted once she realised what he was. Once again the desire for revenge burned bitterly inside her, but it was a revenge she wasn't likely to get, she acknowledged unhappily, unless she planned to return from the dead to haunt him.

So slowly that she hadn't realised it was happening until it was too late, she had come to accept the fact of her own death. Occasionally in a downhearted frame of mind she had contemplated the thoughts that must run through a person's mind when death was imminent, wondering what hers would be, but somehow, even knowing what was going to happen to her it was difficult to focus her thoughts on the actuality of it. Catholics approaching death were bidden to prepare themselves for it, but how did one prepare? Saffron wondered. With prayers? With forgiveness of one's enemies? She wasn't capable of either.

It was almost dawn before she drifted off to sleep, lulling herself into a false sense of security by pretending that she was a small child again held safe in her father's arms.

CHAPTER FIVE

'NOT quite what we're used to, is it?'

Saffron closed her ears to Olivia's insults, recoiling automatically as she always did from the indignity of being watched while she stripped and washed as best she could in the small bowl of water that was supplied. However, this morning there was even more resentment than usual in the Italian girl's voice, and Saffron knew why.

Almost from the moment of her kidnap Olivia had been at pains to imply to Saffron that she and Nico were lovers, but Saffron had sensed early on that the Italian girl was not as sure of Nico as she like to pretend.

'Quite a change for you!' Olivia sneered when Saffron refused to retaliate—she had learned early that to do so merely provoked a blow of some kind from her tormentor and now avoided encouraging her whenever she could. 'Not quite the society lady now, are we? Not many of your fancy men would want you if they could see you now, if it ever was you they wanted and not simply Daddy's money.'

Her last words caught Saffron on a raw spot that had never quite healed. Always at the back of her mind had been the suspicion that some of her acquaintances cultivated her because of who she was rather than any feelings of genuine friendship and she retaliated without thinking, laughing mockingly at Olivia as she asked softly.

'What's the matter? Are you frightened that

Nico might want it too and double-cross you?'

She knew the claim was an outrageous one, but it was worth making it to see the fury in Olivia's eyes just before she launched herself on to Saffron, nails raking her soft skin.

'He wouldn't dare,' she told Saffron. 'The organisation would kill him. He wouldn't want you anyway,' she added scornfully, giving Saffron's hair a vicious tug before thrusting her away so heavily that she half fell to the floor. 'He is just amusing himself with you. He told me about it. 'Just seeing if you are as good in bed as you're supposed to be.'

'And you don't mind? Or is it that you daren't mind?' Saffron suggested shrewdly as she got to her feet. She knew her arrow had found its mark when she saw Olivia's eyes darken, but before she could speak they heard Guido calling from downstairs.

'Be careful!' Olivia muttered as she pushed Saffron out of the room. 'And remember, Nico is mine!'

And she was welcome to him, Saffron told herself fiercely as she walked between the dusty vines, always conscious of Guido behind her, watching her. His unrelenting scrutiny was beginning to unnerve her; he had never made any move to touch her, but she knew that he wanted her; knew and was frightened by the knowledge, sensing something dangerous in him; a similar danger to that of a rabid dog, and her skin crawled every time she felt his eyes on her body, while he boasted of the power of their organisation.

At lunch time she was so hot and tired from bending over the vines that it was a relief when Guido told her to stop work. They were real professionals, she thought tiredly as they headed back to the house, even to the extent of actually working the vines and fields, even though they knew there would not be anyone there to harvest the crop they were raising.

'Perhaps when your *papa* pays us the money I will buy myself a farm like this,' Guido told her as they headed for the farmhouse, 'get myself some land and a plump wife.'

Saffron knew he was baiting her, but still couldn't resist muttering cynically, 'I thought the money was for the cause, whatever that might be.'

She hadn't realised Olivia had caught up with them, her dark eyes flashing ominously as she interrupted furiously, 'Our cause is to cleanse the world of parasites like you; to share out equally its wealth and do away with the corruption of privilege!'

In the valley by the river a sudden movement caught Saffron's eye. She stopped listening to Olivia as she watched Nico emerging from the water, unashamedly naked, his skin gleaming; rivulets of moisture running off the smooth copper shoulders. He had his back to them and Saffron felt her breath catch in her throat as she watched him walk to where he had left his clothes, his body as sleek and fluid as a jungle cat's, oiled skin like satin over hard bones and sinewy muscle.

She must have made some tiny betraying sound, because suddenly Olivia stepped in front of her, raw hatred glittering in her eyes.

'You want him,' she breathed, 'I see it in your eyes, but Nico is mine! See,' she told Guido, 'she lusts after him like a bitch in heat!' Her sneering words were more than Saffron could bear, her emotional reaction to the site of Nico's naked body, something so far outside her normal experience, and so completely devastating that she reacted abnormally, stepping forward, her hand raised . . .

Guido caught it, pulling her arm painfully behind her back, grinning the inane, lustful grin that always brought the tiny hairs on the back of her neck upright in atavistic fear.

'Let me go!' Somehow she managed to twist free, fear lending her the agility to wrest herself from his grasp, something in the way they were both watching her fuelling her earlier dread.

All through lunch she expected to hear Olivia making some contemptuous remark about the brief scene, but to her surprise nothing was said. Olivia spoke more to Piero than Nico, and Saffron wondered if she was trying to make him jealous. There was nothing in his demeanour towards her to suggest that they were lovers, but Saffron suspected that if they weren't they probably had been at one time, and Olivia was desperately hoping for a renewal of their earlier intimacy.

Following the visit by the police Saffron had been allowed a little more freedom; the police were hardly likely to return Nico had said, and there was always at least one person on guard with a gun. Saffron had been told that if she tried to escape she would be shot down, and even though she knew that her death was likely to be the only outcome to her kidnapping, she still couldn't force herself to make the break for it which she *knew* would put an end to her life.

After lunch Nico announced that he had to go into town. Saffron had noticed that he was always the one who made contact with Rome and through them presumably her father, and although she

sensed the others resented it, none of them
questioned his right to do so. He ruled them with
the threat of fear, a despicable weapon, she had
always thought, but obviously a powerful one.

He had been gone about fifteen minutes, and
Saffron had just finished cleaning up after the
meal when Olivia announced that Nico had left
instructions that she was to guard Saffron while
she bathed in the river.

'He said nothing to me,' was her initial reaction,
but Olivia merely sneered, and told her, 'Why
should he? It is not for you to question his orders,
and besides, it will save Piero having to carry up
extra water.'

Saffron admitted to herself that she would
welcome the opportunity to immerse herself fully
and wash away the grime from her skin. The
sketchy washes she had managed with the small
bowls of water she had been brought were better
than nothing, but fell a long way short of bathing.
A delicate flush coloured her skin as she
remembered seeing Nico emerge from the river . . .
the tanned suppleness of his skin, the broad
shoulders tapering to the narrow waist.

The water was every bit as refreshing as she had
imagined. She had forgotten how delicious it felt
to be really, really clean, she thought happily as
she stood breast-high in the water. Olivia had
supplied her with soap and even some shampoo so
that she could wash her hair, still bedraggled from
its enforced cut. Even the coldness of the water
was an invigorating pleasure. A smile curved her
mouth as she reflected how she would have
scorned the very idea that she might find bathing
in a country river a sybaritic luxury as little as a
month ago.

When she stepped out on to the river bank Olivia was nowhere in sight. It was strange for the Italian girl to be less than excessively diligent in her guarding duties, but Saffron was too relieved to be free of her constricting presence to care very much.

She had just started to towel herself dry when a figure emerged from the shadows of the small olive grove. Clutching her towel protectively to her body, Saffron saw Guido moving slowly towards her.

Her first instinct was to run, but fear held her rooted to the spot as he smiled and reached out for her towel.

'Don't bother screaming,' he warned her. 'Olivia won't hear you, and neither will Piero. You shouldn't have made eyes at Nico—Olivia didn't like it.'

And so she had deliberately led her into this trap, Saffron thought numbly, deliberately got her down here, knowing that Guido would find her; knowing that Nico was away . . .

A violent shudder racked her. She turned, a moaned protest escaping bitterly compressed lips, but she wasn't fast enough for Guido. He caught her effortlessly, toying with her like a cat with a mouse, his hands gripping her waist as he let her struggle, his breath hot against her skin as he bent his head towards her.

She would die if he touched her, Saffron thought suffocatingly. She couldn't bear it! His hands were already reaching for her towel, panic and fear making her fight like a terrified animal, her nails raking over his skin, the violence of her rejection catching him off guard so that he was forced to partially release her. Saffron saw his free hand move to his belt, but the significance of his

actions escaped her until she saw the dull blue steel
glint of the knife in his hand.

She shrank from it instinctively, her eyes
repelled and yet glued to the glittering metal. Fear
lodged in a tight lump in her chest, paralysing
thought and movement. Slowly, hypnotically,
Guido moved towards her. All her concentration
was focused on the thin blade glittering malevo-
lently in front of her.

Guido laughed deep in his throat, enjoying her
fear, playing with her as the knife sliced the air in
front of her. Saffron turned, poised to run,
breaking free of the paralysis that gripped her, but
just as she moved Guido reached for her.

'Guido'.

The harsh command splintered the silence,
bringing Saffron's head round jerkily as she
probed the shadows of the grove and saw Nico
running towards them, his mouth a tight line of
fury.

His arrival gave Saffron the courage to fight
against Guido's constraining hold, but she had
misjudged his reaction, his fury at Nico's
obviously unexpected appearance, and he muttered
savagely under his breath as the knife came down,
slashing through her towel, leaving a thin red line
that slowly widened and spread as she stared at it,
red circles whirling like Catherine wheels on Guy
Fawkes' Night, the very last voice she heard was
Nico's, as he snapped, 'Piero, get Guido out of my
sight, otherwise I won't be responsible for what I
might do to him!'

When she came round she was lying in the Land
Rover with someone—Nico, she realised, sitting in
the driver's seat. He was arguing with Olivia,
whose voice was shrill as she demanded angrily,

'Why do you have to take her into town? It's a scratch, that's all!'

'It's a little more than that, Olivia,' Nico replied. 'We don't want her dying on us from septic poisoning, and while we're on the subject, what was she doing alone with Guido in the first place? I gave explicit instructions . . .'

'Perhaps you should have given them to her and not me,' Olivia suggested sulkily.' *Caro*, let me deal with her cut . . . What if she should try to escape while you are in town.'

'She won't,' Nico told Olivia with a quiet confidence that made Saffron shudder, keeping her eyes closed. 'But I have to get that cut seen to. It might need stitching, and she's no use to us dead. Her father is demanding proof that she's alive. Until he gets it, he won't send the money.'

'You said nothing of this before?' It was Piero who muttered the words, Saffron recognised his voice. 'You told us everything is going according to plan.'

'So it is, but you are not so inexperienced in these matters, surely, as not to realise that shrewd businessmen are often just that. In his place I too would demand proof of my daughter's continued existence.'

'So how do we supply it?'

Olivia posed the question.

'She will read a piece from this morning's newspaper—that will convince him.'

'And then he will send the money? This is why you insisted on keeping her alive?'

Nico had insisted! Did that mean the others were pressing for her death already? Pressing her burning face against the hard seat, Saffron tried not to betray the fact that she had regained consciousness.

'It seemed the sensible thing to do.' There was a wealth of world-weariness in Nico's words. 'Rome assured me that you were experienced in these matters,' he added, 'but I find you as careless as untried children. I have to report to them when this mission is completed. Guido has already ignored my instructions once.'

Even without looking at them Saffron could tell that both Piero and Olivia were chastened by his remarks, and even while her situation terrified her, she couldn't help marvelling at Nico's subtle control of the situation and the other members of the gang. He manipulated them like puppets, and yet each one of them individually was a dangerous and highly volatile character. The lure of revenge which had done so much to stop her from completely disintegrating before now seemed to desert her as she contemplated the sheer impossibility of exacting revenge against a man who seemed armoured against anything fate could summon against him. Every man had his Achilles heel, she reminded herself, but something told her one could search a lifetime without finding Nico's weak point.

When Nico finally started the Land Rover engine the vibrations from the ancient vehicle sent such a spasm of pain through her that she lost consciousness again, not coming round until the dusty farm track had been left almost completely behind.

'How do you feel?'

Nico stopped the Land Rover and looked at her. She was still clutching the remnants of the towel round her body, and he frowned as though realising it for the first time.

'Here,' he told her, swiftly removing his shirt, 'you'd better wear this.' He rooted around in the back and produced a pair of clean folded jeans, which he handed to her. 'And these—they'll be far too big, but they're better than nothing. What's the matter now?' he demanded when she simply clutched them and stared numbly at him. 'You won't wear them because they're mine—you'd rather be stark naked, right?'

'I . . . I was wondering if you could possibly turn your back.'

It hurt to say the words, pain grating across her chest, a feeling that her whole body was as fragile as a glass bauble and just as likely to shatter enveloping her.

She was half surprised when Nico did as she had asked, and while she fumbled with buttons and fasteners, blood still seeping slowly from her wound, he said metallically,

'You are aware of what could have happened if I hadn't had to turn back because of a flat tyre, I take it?'

From somewhere she found the courage to reply evenly, 'Yes, Guido would have raped me.'

'Rape? That wasn't the way I heard it. According to Olivia you asked for everything you got.'

'That isn't true!'

'No? You'll be telling me next that you didn't know he wanted you!'

'I . . . I knew.' The quiet words were little more than a whisper. She wasn't going to tell him how Olivia had tricked her, let him think what he liked. She didn't care!

'You knew, and yet you deliberately paraded around in front of him like that?' The harsh, almost flat tone of his voice made her flinch from the bitter cynicism. 'What did you think he was?' he asked angrily. 'One of your tame society escorts? Well, let me enlighten you. To call Guido an animal is doing the jungle kingdom an injustice; you'd be nearer to the mark describing him as a disciple of the Marquis de Sade. However, I'm not naïve, I know quite well that some women find that type of man a turn-on.' He watched Saffron shudder deeply and paused.'Okay, so you're not one of them, but you're experienced enough to know and recognise the type, and knowing, you shouldn't have encouraged him.'

Encouraged him! Tears spurted and she couldn't stop them. 'I didn't!' she told him stormily.

'No?' He grimaced sardonically. 'That's not the way I heard it. You know damn well what effect the sight of your half naked body was likely to have—a man would have to be made of stone not to be turned on by it, and yet you still flaunt yourself . . .'

'Flaunt!' She forget the pain from her wound, and struggled to sit upright. 'I was bathing in the river; I thought Olivia was on the bank. And at least I wasn't parading around completely nude,' she finished in a final exhausting burst of anger which left her face pale and her body trembling with delayed reaction. 'Or doesn't it count when the boot's on the other foot?'

For a moment the gleaming look af amusement in his eyes reminded her of how he had looked the night they met.

'So . . .' he said softly, 'I thought it was you this morning. However, in answer to your question and in my own defence, all I can say is that as yet no woman has been able to commit rape against a man. When that happens you will know that we have true equality of the sexes, but until it does you will simply have to accept the status quo, and the fact that no, it doesn't count.'

It was on the tip of Saffron's tongue to point out to him, as Olivia had drummed into her at every opportunity, that one of the main aims of his organisation was to enforce total equality, but, not for the first time, it struck her that whereas the others never lost an opportunity of singing the praises and parroting the commandments of their organisation, Nico rarely mentioned politics or tried to indoctrinate her as the others had done with their beliefs. In fact in many ways he seemed to remain aloof from his companions. A sudden hole in the road sent her jolting against him, and pain stabbed through her, the thought slipping away as she tried to concentrate on remaining conscious.

CHAPTER SIX

THE cut seeped blood spasmodically all the way to the small town. Nico drove fast but expertly, and although the ancient Land Rover was a far different means of transport from the elegant Mercedes he had hired the first time he had taken her out, as they took the coast road past the villa, Saffron was reminded unbearably of that occasion and the tremulous emotions she had experienced.

All those tender feelings were now dead, trampled underfoot by reality. Once or twice Saffron contemplated throwing herself bodily from the vehicle, but the weakening loss of blood, combined with the strong pressure of Nico's fingers on her arm, acted as a powerful deterrent. The front of his borrowed shirt was now bright scarlet with blood, and she was beginning to feel lightheaded by the time they drove into the small dusty town, so typically Italian with its narrow streets and tall tenement buildings, strewn with lines of washing, grandmothers sitting outside open doors watching over babies, undisturbed by the noise of the Land Rover.

Saffron's heart sank as they drove into what was plainly a poorer part of the town. She had been hoping to warn the doctor that she was being held captive against her will, but these hopes were dashed when Nico pulled up outside a faded stucco building, paint peeling from the walls.

'Dr Michello was once an excellent surgeon, but

unfortunately, he started to drink. If you are thinking of enlisting his aid, let me dissuade you. I shall tell him that you are my wife and your "wound" is the result of a marital tiff. Italy is still very much a male-orientated society; whatever you say to him after that will be discounted as purely female hysteria, even if he is sober enough to understand it. And you'd better put this on,' he added, handing her a lightweight blouson jacket the same shade of grey as his eyes. When he saw how she had to struggle, he helped her on with it as though she were a child, carefully tugging the zip fastener upwards, his knuckled brushing her breasts accidentally and sending strange quivers of sensation shooting through her. She had been colder than she realised and the warmth of the jacket was welcome, especially when she discovered that Nico's prediction concerning the doctor was correct.

He deliberately hurried her past the waiting women, holding her against him so that she was aware of the gun he was concealing beneath his jacket, interrupting the doctor, who was in the middle of talking to one of his patients.

At Nico's insistence they were shown into a shabby treatment room, and Saffron was told to remove her shirt.

She gave Nico a speaking look, and obligingly he turned his back, while the doctor made a surprisingly thorough examination.

'Umm—a clean cut, by the looks of it, and not too deep. I shall give you some ointment to put on it and some pills to take.' He wrote out a prescription which he handed to Nico and then said jovially to Saffron, 'Next time, be nicer to him, mm?'

She had expected Nico to drive back once they had collected the prescription, but to her surprise he parked the Land Rover outside a small hotel, keeping a tight grip on her arm as he helped her out.

'We will stay overnight,' he told her. 'We can make the recording to send to your father, and get Doctor Michello to check on your wound in the morning.'

'Aren't you frightened I might try to escape?' she asked him bitterly, 'with only one of you to guard me?'

'How could you?' His calm infuriated her. 'You have no money, no passport, where would you go? To the police?' He laughed. 'I don't think so.' He patted the slight bulge beneath his jacket meaningfully as they entered the hotel, and still maintaining his grip of her arm approached the desk.

Saffron heard him book a double room in frozen silence, her mind frantically running in exhausting circles trying to seek a means of turning the situation to her advantage. She heard him give his name and then realised that he was passing her off as his wife. She glared at him indignantly, whispering furiously as he manoeuvred her towards the stairs,

'I'm not sharing a room with you . . . I hate you!'

'Don't be naive.' The bored voice was edged with impatience. 'And do not start confusing me with Guido.' She coloured hotly as his disparaging glance slid over her from head to toe. She was still wearing his shirt, as well as his jeans, her hair was clean, but still framed her face in ragged wisps, her skin completely devoid of any make-up.

'No, I suppose you'd prefer Olivia,' she agreed nastily.

His eyebrows rose. 'Would I? Why?'

For a moment she floundered, and then blurted out with a gaucheness that infuriated her, 'Well, she is your . . . your woman, isn't she?'

'Is she?' He looked at her again, and then to her surprise stopped, turned round, and guided her back into the foyer.

Outside, the brilliance of the sunshine after the cool dimness of the hotel blinded her momentarily and she stumbled, fingers clutching at the sinewy strength of his forearm. It was like grasping iron, completely unyielding or giving.

'Where are we going?' She thought Nico must have changed his mind and decided against running the risk of staying in town overnight, but he didn't answer, and she was forced to increase her pace to keep up with his long strides, the pressure of his fingers round her arm in what looked like a casual hold but in reality was anything but, closing over her bones like a vice.

He walked past the Land Rover, and into a part of the town she had not seen before. Monteveno was a town she had never visited on previous trips to the villa. Because it lay inland she had dismissed it as being unworthy of a visit, but now she realised the ancient piazza with its church and medieval buildings was worthy of closer inspection. Nico didn't pause to study the architecture, but headed instead for a small arcade of shops in a shady cloister, stopping outside one of them.

In the window was a plain linen dress, starkly cut and discreetly expensive. To Saffron's surprise Nico marched her into the boutique, speaking to the girl who came to serve them, and gazed at him in appreciatively, in English. To her amazement

Saffron heard them described as holidaymakers, who had come across the town by accident.

'My wife has had a slight accident and needs to replace her . . . blouse,' he explained, and Saffron watched in stupefied silence as several attractive garments were produced for Nico's inspection. His taste was excellent, she admitted grudgingly when he had selected two cotton blouses, one in emerald and the other in a rich lavender, both of which complemented her colouring.

'There is a skirt to match this blouse,' the girl told him, producing a tiered lavender skirt, with a shirred waist designed to fit several sizes.

'We'll take it,' Nico told her, producing a handful of lire notes and the same smile which had once turned Saffron's heart over.

When the girl rang up the cost Saffron moved towards her, but as though he sensed what she was about to do, Nico grasped her arm, his eyes boring warningly into hers as he tapped his breast pocket lightly, and then they were outside on the hot pavement, the moment gone and her resentment burning bright spots of colour along her cheekbones.

Their return to the hotel was accomplished swiftly and effectively. Inside their room Nico produced a paper and the same miniature tape-recorder he had used before,

'Read,' he commanded Saffron expressionlessly, handing her the paper.

For a moment she contemplated refusing, but the futility of it washed over her in depressing waves.

She read for ten minutes before Nico stopped her, playing the tape back before removing it and sealing it in an envelope.

'Good. Perhaps this will encourage your father to make haste. The others are growing impatient.'

'While of course nothing ruffles your patience,' Saffron goaded. 'I'm surprised you didn't want me to make a few realistic screams for added effect.'

She was amazed to see a thin film of brick red colour creep up under his skin. So he was vulnerable after all. She opened her mouth to drive her point home further, when he tossed the blouses and skirt towards her gesturing towards the small bathroom.

'When you are ready call me and I will apply the salve we got from the doctor.'

Saffron stared at him, a curious heat flickering over her skin. The cut was just below her breast, curving through her tender flesh, and something quivered inside her at the thought of having Nico's hands on her body.

'I can do it myself,' she managed jerkily, but his eyebrows lifted contemptuously, his voice edged with malice as he said softly, 'Of course you can, but will you? I wouldn't put it past you to conveniently "forget" and deliberately allow yourself to fall ill and so escape us.'

Her eyes gave her away, and Saffron couldn't deny that the thought had crossed her mind. If she were to fall ill and die and her father were to demand further proof that she was live, she might at least be able to prevent them getting the money.

'So, since I cannot trust you, I shall have to make sure the task is completed myself.'

She was inside the bathroom when he added softly, 'Wear the lavender skirt and blouse. I seem to remember you have particularly attractive legs, as well as other . . . enticing attractions.'

Saffron fully intended to ignore him and dress in

the clothes she had just discarded, but when she emerged from the luxury of a warm shower and picked up his shirt, as well as being stained with her blood, the disturbingly male scent of his body still impregnated the cloth, and she dropped the shirt as though it burned, turning instead to the lavender blouse. It was a wrap-round style with a plunging neckline and tight sleeves, complementing the flounced skirt. The wound showed rawly against her tanned skin, the damp fronds of her butchered hair clinging softly to her face, adding to her fragile appearance, her eyes huge in the delicate oval of her face.

When she stepped into the bedroom, she was trembling with the onset of an emotion she found it hard to decipher. Nico was lounging on one of the beds, reading the paper. He stood up when she walked in, his eyes scrutinising the soft femininity of her body in the lavender shirt and blouse.

'It suits you,' he said at last, 'but I think we can dispense with this if I am to attend to your cut.' He reached deftly for the ties of her blouse, releasing them before Saffron could stop him. Her face flamed and she moved backwards automatically.

Nico ignored the small movement, grasping her shoulder and holding her still while he spread the cream on the throbbing cut. The fingers which had so far merely punished were strangely comforting as they spread the soothing balm against her heated flesh. Strange sensations curled dangerously through her stomach, an odd lassitude enveloped her.

'Saffron?' She caught the hard edge underlining her name, but the room seemed to be tilting oddly, Nico's fingers against her skin the only reality, his eyes dark, and almost concerned as she looked up at him and tried to articulate her concern at the dizzying sickness enveloping her, then Nico and everything else was blotted out as a whirling pool of blackness opened in front of her and she tumbled helplessly into it, sinking drowning . . . floating deliciously on something warm and safe.

The first thing Saffron was aware of when she opened her eyes was her unfamiliar surroundings. She blinked in the strong sunlight streaming in through the uncurtained windows, and glanced slowly round the room. That awful nightmare that she had been kidnapped must have been just that, and yet it had been so real. She frowned as she heard the sound of running water from the bathroom, then her glance fell on to the skirt and blouse she had worn the night before, now neatly folded on a chair, and realisation swept over her and her body tensed beneath the thin sheet.

Her eyes were drawn again to the chair. She couldn't remember undressing herself, which meant . . .

'Good, you're awake.'

She froze, acutely aware of her near-nude state beneath the thin sheet, and blurted out unthinkingly, 'Did you undress me?'

'You passed out, and it seemed a pity to get your finery creased . . . It isn't the first time, and I doubt it will be the last,' he mocked her, 'although normally my women don't pass out on me.'

The laughter in his eyes, and the knowledge that she was his prisoner, combined to form a hard, tight anger.

'I'm not one of your women,' she pointed out freezingly, 'and I object to being classed as one.'

Nico's face hardened, his eyes narrowing as he prised his shoulders away from the door and walked slowly towards the bed, careless of the fact that his only covering was the towel he had knotted round his hips. Saffron tried to drag her eyes away from the raw masculinity of his body, as pagan and malely beautiful as a Greek statue, only unlike marble, his flesh would be warm and responsive to touch.

'So you object, do you?' He was standing beside the bed and Saffron flinched under the cold fury of his eyes. 'Why, I wonder? Because you can't dominate me the way you've dominated your other lovers? Or is it because I get a response from you that they can't?'

'You don't!' She flung the words at him in heated denial without thinking, gasping as the bed depressed under his weight and he pinned her to it, arms either side of her body while he studied her flushed face.

'No?'

There was a wealth of cynical disbelief in the softly spoken word, and Saffron flinched as he bent towards her, turning her head wildly from side to side to escape the punitive force of male lips intent on branding her a liar, as they touched mockingly along the sensitive column of her throat, teasing apart compressed lips and tasting the soft sweetness she had fought to withhold from him with a sensuality that half shocked her.

'Stop acting the virgin!'

The words were more mocking than angry, the hand that had slid beneath the sheet swiftly expert in removing the barrier of her bra. Saffron tried to protest when the sheet was pushed aside, modesty outraged by the lazy appreciation in his dark grey eyes as they made a thorough inspection of creamy white flesh which had never been touched by the sun and rosy pink nipples.

'Clever girl,' he admired. 'Total nudity lacks challenge, and you have obviously learned that a man wants most what he must fight to obtain. That pale band of flesh suggests a modesty we both know you don't possess, and yet even knowing I find it very erotic to think I am seeing something that has been hidden from others. Very erotic,' he reaffirmed huskily, his fingers stroking slowly over the curves of her breasts and causing tiny spirals of pleasure to curl insidiously through her body. Against her will she was responding to him, and there was nothing she could do about it, Saffron thought bitterly. This was the price she paid for being inexperienced; if she had had the many lovers he had suggested she might have some inkling of how to preserve a cool façade; indeed, she might not need to—surely a woman of experience could not be as vulnerable to a single caress as she was to Nico's?

'You're trembling.'

'Because I hate you so much,' she told him. 'Hate and loathe you.'

'You do?' Amusement masked the anger glowing darkly in his eyes, but Saffron only had a moment to wonder why he should be so angry before his mouth came down on hers, hard hands trapping her head so that she was powerless to move. She moaned protestingly deep in her throat, straining to push him away, but Nico was too strong for her. Her small fists were captured, the fingers spread and placed against his skin, the roughness of male body hair tingling against her soft palms. Against her will she felt a response stir deep inside her, and as though he sensed what she was feeling the bruising pressure of his mouth eased as Nico teased and stroked her lips into soft surrender, small moans of pleasure lost against his throat as his lips moved slowly over her skin, tracing her collarbone, and then moving downwards to where his fingers still caressed the hardening peaks of her breasts.

Molten fire erupted inside her, a feverish need clamouring through her body. Beneath her lips his skin tasted salty and male, and oddly vulnerable. She could see the darkened colour tinging his cheekbones, his eyes dark with sexual desire.

'Nico . . .' His name shivered past her lips, a plea for mercy, and a cry for fulfillment, and a shockwave of rejection shuddered through her as she felt him stiffen and slowly release her.

'You'd better get dressed. We've got to get back.' The flatly spoken words and the coldly dismissive curve of his back as he turned away from her were like a physical blow. She wanted to rage and scream, to . . . To what? she asked herself bleakly; demand that he gave her the fulfillment her body was now craving? Sickness clawed at her stomach. What sort of woman was she? Always she had prided herself on her fastidiousness, on her refusal to indulge in sex for sex's sake, for cheap thrills, and yet here she was suffering the most acute pangs of sexual frustration over a man she loathed and despised. What was happening to her? She had read stories of the bitterly intense relationships that developed between captor and kidnapped; perhaps now she was experiencing them at first hand. She stole a glance at Nico's impassive back through downcast lashes, shuddering with the realisation of how he had

awakened her senses to sensuality. Before, the
male body had held no attractions for her; now
she longed to touch the smooth skin of his back
and feel his muscles clench in a need as great as
her own; and yet she hated him. She ought to
despise herself, but somehow her overriding
emotion was one of frustration that he had turned
his back on her. He got up and picked up his shirt,
pulling it on, his hands reaching for the towel
wrapped round him. Saffron touched her tongue
to hot, dry lips, her eyes mesmerised by the taut
suppleness of his body.

'I'm not the sideshow!'

The terse words shocked her into awareness,
and the air left her lungs on a painful hiss as she
dragged her eyes away,

'Here, take these and get dressed.'

She turned just in time to catch the clothes Nico
threw her, her face scarlet as she realised her
sudden movement had exposed the top half of her
body, but unlike her, he seemed to have no
inclination to let his eyes linger and grabbing the
skirt and blouse, Saffron hurried into the
bathroom the moment he turned his back.

When she re-emerged she found that breakfast
had been brought to the room. The coffee tasted
delicious after the food they had been eating at the
farmhouse, and she drank several cups, before she
realised that Nico had finished his breakfast and
was waiting for her. Absurdly she wanted to
prolong her time with him but there was nothing
absurd about her reluctance to return to the
farmhouse. She shivered, remembering what
waited for her there.

'Come on. You've got to see the doctor and I
want to send this tape off to your father. So far

he's done everything we've told him, for your sake I hope he continues to do so.'

The doctor gave her cut a cursory glance and told Nico that it was healing well. He had insisted on accompanying her into the doctor's surgery, telling Saffron blandly that the doctor would see nothing odd in his determination. 'Italian men are loath to leave their women alone with other males, the good doctor will quite understand why I don't want him to be alone with my beautiful wife.'

Strangely enough that taunt hurt more than anything else that had happened to her. She knew she looked far from beautiful with her cropped hair and make-upless face; there was no need for Nico to rub salt in the wound and mock her for her lack of femininity.

Once outside he directed her steps towards the piazza where he had bought her clothes, never releasing his firm grip of her arm. Under her lashes Saffron watched him, wondering about him; about the events that had brought him to his present situation. He was plainly well educated and intelligent; he spoke English fluently and was far less volatile than she would have expected for an Italian. That he could control the other members of the gang was self-evident, and that in itself was no easy task, so qualities of leadership and diplomacy must be added to undeniable charm and shrewdness. Surely such a man could have made his mark in any number of legitimate careers, so why had he chosen to live outside the law? Was it the challenge of living in such close contact with danger; or was it simply the money that appealed to him? The answer was something she was never likely to know, Saffron decided, as he drew her into a small building which she realised belatedly was the post office.

Watching him post the tape to her father she was filled with an overwhelming sense of homesickness. Tears welled up in her eyes and refused to be blinked away, and to her intense chagrin several escaped to trickle bleakly down her face.

'Here.'

She took the handkerchief and dried her eyes, and as her vision cleared she saw that two police officers had entered the building. Nico had released her while she dried her eyes, and acting impulsively, she started to run forward, all her hopes and determination concentrated on reaching the policemen by the door.

She had a few seconds' start on Nico and for a moment she thought it was going to be enough. Being small she could dart among the other customers, which he could not, but just as she reached her goal she felt his hands closing on her body, jerking her backwards, his face a mask of cold fury as he swung her round to face him, so hard that she almost lost her balance.

The policemen looked up; several other people were staring at them. Saffron opened her mouth to beg for help, and cried out with pain instead as Nico's hand left its impact on her face.

For the second time he physically chastised her, although this time somehow the pain wasn't as great, shock being her overriding reaction, for powerful though the blow had looked in reality it had done little more than stun her into silence.

'She has been seeing another man,' he explained for the benefit on the curious police. 'My cousin, no less, and when I tax her with it, she denies it, when all my village have seen them together!'

The police laughed and made a comment that brought fresh colour to Saffron's cheeks; their earthy humour not to her liking. Or course Italy was a male-dominated country, she remembered bitterly, where a man could openly chastise his wife without anyone thinking to interfere, and southern Italy, less sophisticated than the north, still looked upon a wife as her husband's chattel.

With a grip that bruised, Nico marched her back outside, not stopping until they had rounded the corner and were in sight of the Land Rover.

'Try anything like that again and it will be a bullet you'll feel, instead of the flat of my hand. Hell, but you try my patience, you really do! What did you hope to gain?"

'The most precious thing in the world,' Saffron told him tautly, 'my freedom.'

'Is that why you have never married?' he asked her, catching her off guard. 'Because your "freedom" means too much to you?'

Saffron shrugged. 'Aren't you being a little naïve?' she taunted mockingly, salving her pride for the blow he had inflicted upon it. 'If one really wants to one can find all the freedom one desires within marriage these days . . .'

'So . . .' He shrugged, 'perhaps you couldn't find anyone willing to take you on, on those terms, shopsoiled as you are, so to speak . . .'

'Shopsoiled! Haven't you ever heard of female equality?' she demanded. 'Not all men want timid little virgins in their beds.'

'Not in their beds,' Nico agreed suavely. 'But as their wives . . . that's a different matter.'

His complacency infuriated her; she could have told him that she hadn't married because she cherished a ridiculous dream of finding a man she could respect and honour as well as love; a man who could be a man and encourage her to be a woman without dominating her or wanting to put her down. She had begun to think such men did not exist.

The drive back to the farmhouse was uneventful, although with every mile that took her closer to her prison, Saffron's feeling of terror which had begun in Monteveno built up until by the time they actually reached their destination she could think of nothing but the proximity of her own death.

Her life span was only as long as her father's search for the ransom money, she was sure of that. Once they knew it was going to be paid over, she would be disposed of without mercy. Why else would they allow her to see and possibly later identify them? They must think she was a fool, she thought bitterly, especially Nico, who was amusing himself with her, playing with her emotions, knowing what her ultimate fate was to be.

Olivia greeted them with sullen silence. There was a livid bruise along Guido's jaw, and a savage anger in his eyes when he looked at them which intensified Saffron's fear. Only Piero seemed unchanged.

'Have you sent the tape?'

Olivia was openly truculent, her eyes constantly searching Saffron's face, although looking for what Saffron neither knew nor cared. She had already noticed the skirt and blouse Saffron was wearing, and when Nico had aswered her she added aggressively, 'You let her go into a shop alone? Wasn't that taking a risk, or does she have some reason for staying with us that the rest of us know nothing about?'

Saffron's colour rose in spite of her determination not to react to the other girl's malice.

'Neither,' Nico drawled, without looking at Saffron. 'I bought them for her. The things she was wearing were practically in rags,' he added smoothly before Olivia could object. 'I decided to replace them in case they drew attention to us. No one queries the presence of two foreigners obviously on holiday, but the sight of a man with a girl at his side, dressed in rags, is bound to be remembered by someone.'

It was obvious that Olivia wasn't happy with the situation and equally obvious that she could think of no further criticisms to overset the logic of Nico's argument. Saffron couldn't herself. Ever since she had woken up in the morning she had been beset by conflicting feelings over which she had no control. There had been a look in Nico's eyes this morning—anger mingled with something else; an almost unwilling admiration combined with self-contempt. If she hadn't known better she might almost have supposed that he was regretting his part in her kidnapping—and yet she couldn't be the first victim he had been involved with in this way; and she couldn't flatter herself that his feelings towards her were likely to be any different than to any of the others.

The evening meal was a silent affair, with Olivia constantly glancing from Nico to Saffron, her eyes watchful and angry. Nico must be aware of her feelings, Saffron knew, and yet he appeared not to notice the furious looks she was giving him, and she wondered at his attitude, especially when as leader he must be conscious of the need to preserve an amicable relationship between the other members of the gang and himself. After the meal

was over Saffron noticed how Olivia went straight
to Guido's side and how they both stood talking in
low voices as Nico studied the paper he had
bought in town, and Saffron herself cleared the
table under Piero's watchful eyes.

'Leave that,' Nico told her when the things were
washed and she started to dry them. 'Olivia and
Guido can finish them.' The glance he threw the
duo in the corner was cynically assessing. 'How's
your cut?' he asked Saffron abruptly. 'Are you
taking the prescription?'

She nodded in confirmation. The cut was
healing quite well, but Nico's apparent concern
unnerved her. Why was he showing such a belated
interest in her welfare? Was he trying to lull her
into a false sense of security for some
Machiavellian purpose of his own? Did he get some
sort of kick out of coaxing her to trust him and then
destroying that trust? she wondered bitterly.

Four days had passed since Nico had taken her
into the town, and Saffron was discovering that
the mood of her captors had begun to change
dangerously. Whenever they quoted the maxims
of the organisation to her now, it was always
with a bitterly vitriolic denunciation of her own
culture—a culture they were pledged to destroy.
But it was their fanatical hatred of the Roman
Catholic Church Saffron found the most terrifying.
According to them, it was going to be their first
target for destruction, and Saffron shuddered
when Olivia turned on her one morning saying
savagely, 'Religion has been the opiate of the
masses for too long—they are deluded and
deceived into believing that there is better to come;
that "heaven" awaits them, and because they in

their folly have believed it they have become slaves to religion. And why have we not yet heard from her father?' she demanded of Nico. 'There has been time enough. Perhaps he does not yet take our threats seriously,' she added. 'We have never had these delays in the past.'

'We are now living in the present,' Nico told her smoothly. 'And you know the orders from Rome. I am in charge of this operation.'

'Olivia is right,' Piero cut in angrily. 'Perhaps it is time we tried to speed matters up a little. We cannot remain here in safety very much longer.'

'I say we should send her father something to remind him how vulnerable his daughter is,' Olivia suggested. 'Perhaps we should remind him of the blood tie by sending him something a little more tangible than simply a taped message. The Getty boy was ransomed quickly enough once his family received . . .'

'Enough! I will not listen to any more!' Nico commanded. 'I am in charge of this operation and I shall be the one to decide what steps we take and when, and you will all follow my orders!'

Silence fell as they listened to him, and a nauseous dread clawed at the pit of Saffron's stomach as she contemplated Olivia's threat.

How would they mutilate her? By removing her finger, her ear? The mere thought was enough to bring her out in an ice-cold sweat, but she refused to give in to it, or to give Olivia the satisfaction of seeing her react to the other girl's suggestion.

She knew all about what had happened to Paul Getty's grandson; she had seen it in the papers and remembered her father commenting on it, although she had only been young at the time. His captors had cut off his ear and sent it to his family. And it hadn't been the only case of mutilation. But then he had been ransomed and had lived! If only she could escape! But how? Escape was impossible, she knew that and yet still she yearned for it, was obsessed by it.

And now she was faced with the threat which Olivia had just made. It terrified her, adding a new dimension to the fear she was already experiencing.

The day dragged on. Twice Saffron saw Olivia and Guido closeted together as they worked, talking in low whispers. Were they planning to ignore Nico's commands, usurp his authority even? She had sensed in Olivia a change, a hardening towards Nico and a reluctance to accept his word as law. Somehow he had become her only protection against Olivia's malice and Guido's lechery, and she grew fearful every time he disappeared from sight, worrying about what might happen to him. She didn't put it past Olivia to carry out her gruesome promise of mutilation without Nico's authority—after all, what could he do once it was accomplished? She tried not to picture her father's agony if he were to receive such evidence of her plight.

She couldn't touch her evening meal, her movements were listless and uncaring. Once or twice she felt Nico's gaze, but refused to look at him.

When he rose from the table, abruptly, pushing back his chair with the first awkward movement she had seen him make her eyes flew instinctively to his.

'Piero, our guest looks as though she could do with some fresh air. Walk with her as far as the river and back.'

'Not taking her yourself?' Olivia questioned

maliciously. 'Don't tell me she turned you down?'

The Italian girl's desire seemed to have turned to dislike in a remarkably short space of time, Saffron reflected as she followed Piero outside, or was it simply that Olivia was masking her true feelings with pretended contempt?

Darkness had already fallen, but the subtropical night air was soft and warm, the thought of being locked up in her small room once her walk was over causing feelings of acute claustrophobia. In any other circumstances the walk through the olive grove to the river would have been very pleasant, but with Piero at her back, ready to pounce on her the moment she set a foot wrong, much of the pleasure was dissipated.

All she possessed was the illusion of freedom, and it could never be any substitute for the real thing. Ahead of them the river gleamed silver-black under the hunter's moon, and stars shimmered in the midnight blue sky.

Saffron walked along the river bank for several yards, stopping abruptly as she recognised Nico walking towards them from the opposite direction. Obviously he too had wanted to breathe in the soft night air, but unlike her he was free to do so whenever he wished. Her lips twisted bitterly at the thought.

'Piero, I want you to take a look at the Land Rover,' Nico told the other man as he drew abreast of them. 'The engine's running hot.'

'I'll give it a test run now,' Piero suggested, 'and then I can go over it in the morning.'

'Fine. We don't want to risk being without it.'

As Piero slipped away into the darkness and they were left alone, a curious constraint came over Saffron. She glanced out across the river, yearningly, bitterly resentful of Nico's touch on her arm, telling her that it was time to go back. Behind her lay the farmhouse and imprisonment, in front of her the river, and then freedom.

An instinct that overwhelmed caution and fear swept over her, and then without conscious thought she was turning and running, not towards the farmhouse, but away from it, towards the river, no conscious plan formulated in her mind, only a desperate need to be free.

She had caught Nico off guard, and heard him curse softly behind her, but she closed her ears against the sounds of pursuit. Lungs and heart pounding to the point of bursting, she willed her body into a speed she had not known since schooldays. Her enforced captivity had made her lose weight, but that only gave her a momentary advantage; Nico had the strength and stamina she lacked, and behind her she could hear unmistakably that he was gaining on her.

Even then, knowing what the outcome must be, she refused to give in, punishing her body until it screamed in protest, not caring that she was driving herself to the point of collapse, the only thought in her throbbing head the need to escape, to sink into the ground and become absorbed in it, part of it—*free*!

CHAPTER SEVEN

SUDDENLY she was falling ... falling, to hit the
ground with a thud that jarred her teeth and drove
the breath from her lungs. A heavy weight pinned
her to the ground. She lifted her head in exhausted
defeat and stared ahead of her to where the river
ran smoothly between its banks.

'Little fool!' The harsh condemnation was laced
with anger. Dragging air into her tortured lungs in
aching gasps, Saffron lay quiescent as Nico turned
her over on to her back, arms falling uselessly to
her side, her whole body shivering with reaction.
'What did you hope to gain?'

'Freedom!' The word was thick and slurred with
pain, defeat etched into her face as the moonlight
slid over it, mercilessly revealing her anguish.
Above her she heard Nico curse, and then,
unbelievably, he was cupping her face, kissing her
with a heated urgency that melted her body and
left her strangely fluid and receptive to his touch.
This was no exploratory embrace, no cynical
punishment, but the touch of a man driven beyond
the bounds of self-imposed restraint into an action
of explosive need, and Saffron's senses recognised
it as such. The moon slid behind a cloud; with
preternaturally heightened senses she could hear
the soft movements of the river, the whispers of
the night all around them, and a wild clamouring
swirled through her, a desperate need to experience
all life's pleasures before it was too late; without
conscious thought she rejected the code by which she

118

had previously lived her life. If she was going to die
she wanted to experience life first; to know the desire
and possession of a man, even if that man was her
captor, or so her body reasoned, and she could no
longer fight against it. There seemed to be a strange
sort of fatality about being here with Nico, as
though it was something that had long ago been
ordained there was nothing she could do about it.

Her arms lifted to his shoulders, her mouth
parting to his kiss. There was nothing tentative
about his touch; it was that of a man aroused to
the point where nothing mattered save the need to
assuage his desire. Saffron felt it in the hard
urgency of his mouth and the tautness of the male
thighs pinning her to the ground.

The buttons on her blouse gave way beneath his
impatient fingers, and the new, unknown Saffron
who seemed to have been born in the moments of
her defeat when she tried to escape from him felt
only a thrill of pleasure at the way Nico exposed
her body to the moonlight and studied it fixedly
while the silence thickened around them.

'In this light your skin could almost be
alabaster,' he muttered feverishly. 'You could have
modelled for a statue of Diana. But your flesh is
warm with the temptation of a newly ripened
peach, and just looking at you brings out a pagan
need in me to touch and taste.'

He bent his head, and something sweet and
languorous curled headily through her veins. The
touch of his tongue as it stroked across the
budding tips of her breasts was a delight and a
torment, provoking a muscle-clenched reaction,
and a wanton impulse which she didn't deny to
lock her fingers in the dark disorder of his hair
and hold his head against her skin.

Only the fine tremble of Nico's body betrayed his own reaction, but the heat coming off his skin and the low groan that escaped his lips as they moved in hungry possession against her breast showed that she was not alone in her need to submit to the magic of the night.

When Nico removed her skirt she felt only heady pleasure because it allowed her closer contact with his body. She had already unfastened his shirt, but when he pulled it off completely, followed by his jeans, she drew in her breath in wonder at the male perfection of his body.

'Don't just look at me, touch me,' he muttered thickly, lowering his body to meet hers, circling her with his arms, as his mouth explored her skin. The barriers of shyness and inexperience were swept away, her response total as she pressed trembling lips to male flesh that shuddered to her touch, and yet incited it to be repeated.

Something in their mutual desire sparked off a fevered, almost frantic response in Saffron; a need to drink deeply, knowing that the cup of life was about to be dashed from her lips before she had even tasted the bitter-sweet wine of love.

She felt Nico's full weight on top of her, the tautness of his muscles and the aroused maleness of his body.

'Why?' he demanded softly against her lips. 'Why now and not before?'

She knew what he meant, and with all the barriers down between them could answer him honestly.

'Perhaps because I want to experience everything life has to offer before it's too late.'

She felt him pause, probing the darkness,

turning her face into the moonlight to search it feature by feature with eyes suddenly cool and wary.

'I think I heard you, but tell me again, just to make sure I'm not imagining things.'

Hesitantly Saffron did so. When she had finished there was silence. And then Nico said flatly, 'Are you trying to tell me you're still a virgin?'

'And if I am?' Why did her voice have to tremble over the words?

He sighed, and straightened up, sitting with his back to her so that she couldn't read his expression. Then he reached for his jeans.

'Now I've heard everything,' he said wryly. 'But something tells me you aren't lying. Is this honestly what you want?' he demanded curtly. 'A purely physical coming together with a man you don't even know? If it is, why not before? Why now?'

'Because you're here,' Saffron replied as calmly as she could, glad of the darkness to hide her features. This wasn't the response she had envisaged. Nico was lecturing her like an irate parent. She climbed into her clothes again.

'So are Guido and Piero,' he told her evenly. 'Are you saying that they would have done equally well?'

She wanted to, but somehow couldn't force the lie between her lips. Nico had turned round and was studying her, so she shook her head mutely.

'Saffron.' He placed his hands on her shoulders and looked down into her face. It was the first time she could remember him using her name and it added an almost unbearable note of intimacy to the proceedings.

'You might be innocent and naïve, but not so much that you won't realise the truth of what I'm about to say. Situations such as this one act like hothouses, forcing the emotions and channelling them in ways they wouldn't normally be channelled—hence the events of tonight.' He paused and seemed to grimace a little in distaste, and a sense of rejection shocked and hurt her as she realised that he was not, after all, going to make love to her.

'If you didn't want me, why did you start making love to me in the first place?' she managed, holding on to her pride, and trying to avoid the look in his eyes.

'I wanted what I thought was an equally experienced and worldly woman,' Nico corrected her brutally, 'not an inexperienced girl child who was using me merely to further her education. You should be grateful,' he added tersely. 'This way you get to save it all for the purpose it is obviously intended for—the sanctity of the marriage bed!'

'Which I'm not now likely to have,' Saffron pointed out bitterly. 'And anyway, I wasn't saving myself for that.'

'No?'

The mockery in the word infuriated her.

'No,' she retorted heatedly.

'Then what, or rather who?'

For a moment she was tempted not to answer, but something deep inside her overruled her innate disinclination to reveal her most private thoughts and feelings, so in a low voice she said hesitantly, 'Someone I could respect and trust as well as desire physically, and who felt the same way about me; a total commitment and involvement of mind and body, a . . .'

'Soulmate,' Nico supplied wryly. 'But in the end reality fell very far short of your ideal, or would have done had I not stopped. Oh, come,' he drawled when she made no response, 'surely you are not going to tell me that your virginal heart yearned to cast me in the role of perfect lover, a shining white knight, whose perfection was almost divine.'

His mockery stung and she retaliated bitterly, 'Needs must when the devil drives, and faced with . . .'

'Going to your grave an innocent or taking me as your first lover you chose, the latter,' Nico supplied harshly. 'Am I supposed to be flattered? If so I'm afraid I must disappoint you, and a word of advice—next time you respond so passionately to a man by way of an experiment do him the favour of pandering to his ego and keeping it a secret.'

'Nico!' Olivia emerged from the shadows, calling his name, and Nico turned to help Saffron to her feet. Her skin burned at his touch, but he seemed unaware of anything intimate in the brief contact of flesh on flesh.

'Oh, there you are,' the other girl exclaimed unnecessarily. 'We thought something must have happened, you were so long.'

'Nothing happened,' Nico assured her, and the words were like a pain in Saffron's heart. Nothing might have happened to him, but to her . . . Rejection was no easy thing to bear, especially when the one doing the rejecting was a man she had sworn hatred and vengeance against.

Confused and bewildered by her own emotions, she started to walk back to the farmhouse. With the cooling evening breeze blowing over her skin the frenzied desire she had experienced in Nico's arms seemed to have been felt by another person, like a dream incompletely remembered. It seemed impossible to believe that she actually behaved in that way, responded so passionately, and yet deep down inside her there was still a tiny ache of regret, a thought that 'if only' she had not spoken when she had . . . Banishing the traitorous thought to the back of her mind, she entered the farmhouse and walked upstairs to her room, the malevolence of Olivia's darkly bitter gaze an almost physical emotion in the small, confined room.

'How much longer do we have to stay here?' she heard the Italian girl demanding of Nico, when she was secured in her room and Olivia had returned downstairs. 'They must be growing impatient in Rome. We have never taken so long to complete a mission before.'

'No,' Nico agreed, as Saffron strained to catch his deeper, softer voice, 'and you have never been so close to capture as you were last time. That was a foolish thing you did, killing John Hunter when you did. It lost us the ransom, too.'

'The police were on to us.' Saffron could hear Olivia's voice quite clearly. 'He had seen us and could describe us, we couldn't afford to take risks.'

The days had taken on a dreary routine. After breakfast Saffron worked in the fields, always under the keen eye of one of her gaolers. Nico drove most days into the local town; sometimes Olivia went with him, sometimes one of the others, and she had learned to tell herself that the pain she felt when she saw him with Olivia meant nothing. How could she feel anything for him after all? He had humiliated her, betrayed her trust, hurt her physically and mentally, and done them all with a hard determination against which her puny retaliatory blows wounded no one but herself.

Today dull clouds lay heavily on the horizon, threatening rain, and as the day wore on and the light breeze dropped the electric tension presaging the coming storm seemed to infiltrate the farmhouse as well.

Tempers were on edge, Olivia snapping at Guido and Piero over lunch. Piero barely reacted, concentrating on his pasta, but Guido took her roughly by the arm, shaking her almost violently. Olivia pulled away, tension crackling between them, and in the stormy atmosphere Saffron felt her wound ache for the first time. It had healed well, but she suspected there was always be a faint scar just below the curve of her breast to remind her of what had happened—as though she needed any reminding.

Nico had gone into town, and rather than endure the atmosphere in the farmhouse Saffron walked outside. Piero followed her, leaning against the second Land Rover, cleaning his gun as he watched her, a silent warning that she would be foolish to ignore. How quickly the human mind adapted, she thought wretchedly as she followed the dusty track down to the olive grove. Already she found nothing odd in the sight of guns; in the fact of being a prisoner.

Alone in the grove the thoughts that had been building up all day overwhelmed her. Why hadn't her father been in contact with the gang? Was it simply that he was having trouble raising such a large sum of money, as she had suspected he would, or had Olivia been right, didn't he care if didn't get her back? Tears formed, but she didn't let them fall. Her father loved her, and she would cling to that thought no matter what.

The lack of communication from her father seemed to affect everyone's nerves, not just her own.

'He is just toying with us,' Olivia burst out, eyeing Saffron venemously, 'and you are encouraging him, Nico. With every day that passes there is a greater risk of us being discovered. We must leave here.'

'No!' Guido frowned angrily at Olivia. 'If we leave we draw attention to ourselves. We must see it through now.'

'But we cannot wait here for ever,' Olivia pointed out. 'We must do something. Sir Richard needs something to remind him of the danger to his daughter's existence.'

Saffron shrank visibly under the renewed threat of mutilation. Hearing it once had terrified her into making a hopeless bid for freedom, and since then it had not been mentioned.

'No!' Nico looked and sounded abrupt, his expression grimly withdrawn. Was he angry with Olivia because she kept questioning his orders? 'I have already told you no, once; I do not believe Sir Richard is delaying through any ulterior motive. A million pounds takes some raising even for the wealthy, especially when it must be done with stealth. He has asked for a little more time, and I am disposed to grant it.'

'While we kick our heels here, running the risk of being discovered with every day that passes!' Olivia spat.

'You are not thinking properly,' Nico criticised, apparently uncaring of the vitriolically angry glare

Olivia gave him. 'If we were to take the sort of action you suggest now, personally I am convinced that Sir Richard wouldn't hesitate to call in the police. We are not dealing with a fool, Olivia.'

'And Rome?' she goaded. 'What do they have to say about this? They cannot be pleased with you, Nico.'

'On the contrary, they have a far more realistic view of life than you, *cara mia*. They are quite content to leave matters in my hands—but you are perfectly welcome to take the matter up with them if you wish.'

The uneasy glances exchanged by Olivia and Guido made Saffron wonder if their attack on Nico's leadership had perhaps been preplanned. There had been a shift in loyalties among the members of the gang, with Olivia and Guido markedly turning to one another.

'I have to go to Rome anyway,' Nico announced, shocking them all. 'While I am gone you will do nothing to prejudice our position. When I return we can discuss the matter again if we have not heard from Sir Richard during that time. If any one of you ignores my orders you will have to face me personally when I return—I hope I make myself clear?'

It was apparent that he did, and not for the first time Saffron marvelled at his control of them. For a moment she longed to beg him to take her with him, not to leave her alone with the others, but what was the point? She knew he would refuse, and anyway, wasn't he as equally to be abhorred as the others? There was no difference between them except that Nico had the greater control over his emotions and reactions.

Half an hour later he had gone. Saffron did her

usual stint in the fields watched over by Piero and subject to a forceful lecture of the evils of a capitalistic state. She ignored it as she had started to ignore all their tirades. Initially she had listened closely, hoping that by doing so she might come to have a closer understanding of them, but their blindness to the flaws in the doctrines of their organisation made it impossible for her to even discuss the subject with them.

She had lost weight during her enforced imprisonment; her skin had been tanned even darker by the strong sun, and it was so long since she had worn make-up that she was quite used to the sight of herself without mascara or lipstick. Her butchered hair had grown a little and curled delicately round her face, the elfin locks making her eyes seem huge in her fragilely boned face.

'You are here to work, not daydream!'

She hadn't seen Olivia approach and straightened her aching back as the Italian girl strode towards her, one hand resting aggressively on her hip while the other held her gun.

'You may deceive Nico, but you don't deceive me,' Olivia continued derisively. 'You hope that by sharing your bed with him you will encourage him to be lenient with you, but it won't work. Rome would never tolerate it. Even if Nico wanted to favour you he would never dare. The organisation never forgives treachery from one of its members, and Nico knows that, so you are not as clever as you believe. Oh, he will take what you offer,' she sneered. 'He will enjoy your body, but that is all. When he returns he will see things our way. You may think you can sway him with your body, but you will see. You had better start praying that your father raises that money soon,' she finished threateningly. 'Don't deceive yourself that Nico cares for you as a person. He despises you and your sort, as we all do.'

'You're saying that because you're jealous,' Saffron retorted.

She had said the words on impulse, but knew that she had guessed correctly and that against all logic Olivia was jealous of her.

'You are lying!' Olivia hissed at her. 'Nico takes you simply because your eyes beg him to, and above all else he is very much a man . . . but that is all you are to him—a body!'

Saffron mulled over Olivia's words later in the day, and wondered what the other girl would have done if she had told her the truth—that Nico had rejected her. Nico, Nico . . . why must he occupy so many of her thoughts? she asked herself resentfully; thoughts that should be fully occupied in finding a way out of her present situation. She tried to concentrate on her father, on the routine of his day, wondering what he was feeling and thinking at this very moment. Was she in his thoughts? Was he regretting his decision not to go to the police, or was he frightened that by doing so he would be prejudicing her position? How would he raise the money? She knew he did not possess so much cash and to realise it would mean realising many of his assets—the Impressionist paintings he had collected so lovingly over the years, the antiques chosen by her mother, perhaps even selling some shares in the company, and surely none of this could be done quickly or without causing suspicion?

The storm which had been threatening broke that evening, thunder and lightning filling the sky. Saffron went to bed with a tense headache, glad to escape the atmosphere in the room below. Guido had been giving her hotly lustful glances all evening, and she felt frighteningly vulnerable without Nico to act as a bulwark against the other man's lust for her.

Dawn came with a fresh clarity after the storm. Saffron could hear Piero whistling downstairs. When eventually Olivia came to release her she had not brought the normal bowl of water. When Saffron commented on it the other girl remarked bitchily, 'What's the matter, don't you think Nico will want you if you aren't all delicately perfumed? Nico is a man,' she told Saffron scornfully, 'and prefers a real woman to some spoiled, pampered Daddy's darling!'

As the days had gone by, and her captors had grown less concerned about the danger of being discovered, they had become less cautious about allowing Saffron any freedom. 'Where could she go to?' Olivia asked scornfully, when Piero barred her way through the door. 'And how? as Piero himself had the only set of keys for the second Land Rover. 'Let her go,' she told Piero. 'You can watch her from here. If she starts to run, shoot her.'

Saffron didn't make the mistake of thinking she was merely making an idle threat. The river drew her, although she was unwilling to admit the reason why. She stood watching it for several minutes, and then on a sudden impulse removed her blouse and shabby jeans and paddled into the water, not stopping until it was waist-high. As before, the luxury of feeling clean again was something she revelled in, although this time she was careful to keep an eye on the river bank and did not stay too long in the water. She had no towel to dry herself on, but the sun would soon dry her damp underwear. She could see Piero up at the farmhouse, but her underwear was as respectable as many bikinis—more so, in fact, and this was the time of the day when Guido would have driven down to the village to collect their stores. One of them went into the village every few days, their presence now accepted without any comment.

When she returned to the farmhouse the Land Rover was parked outside, but there was no sign of Guido. Thinking that he was out with the vines, Saffron stepped unsuspectingly into the dimness of the room.

A hand shot out to circle her throat choking the breath out of her lungs, garlic-laden breath mingled with the sourness of wine breathed close to her ear, as Guido warned, 'Don't struggle,' and then his free hand was on her body, ripping off the buttons of her blouse in his haste, his touch scorching her skin as she saw the burning lust in his eyes, and knew that he had deliberately lain in wait for her. All the fear she had ever experienced before was as nothing compared with the impending violation of her body. Every muscle screamed its distraught protest, her eyes those of a terrified hunted animal as Guido bent his head and the hot wetness of his mouth closed sickeningly over hers.

Saffron fought like a trapped creature, finger-nails raking his face, but her blows seemed only to amuse him. Her blouse was wrenched from her body, his hand probing the flimsy protection of her bra while she shrank under his touch. Unlike Nico there was no lean male scent to his skin, rather the rank, sour odour of a wild animal.

Gagging with nausea, Saffron felt his hands on her body, through the swirling red mist of terror and pain she heard a door slamming and then voices.

'Guido, let go of her!'

Nico! She sagged weakly with relief, but Guido, maddened with lust, refused to heed Nico's command.

'Let her go, I said!'

'And I am tired of doing what you say!' With a brutal hand Guido thrust Saffron to the floor, his knife appearing like magic, glittering evilly as he advanced on Nico.

Saffron's fear for herself was submerged beneath her terror for Nico. He was unarmed, while Guido had his knife. She knew beyond logic than neither of the others would help Nico, that was what happening in front of her was the culmination of more than simply Guido's desire for her and Nico's thwarting of it, and she shivered convulsively as the two antagonists converged, Guido's hand describing a swift arc as the knife swept downwards.

Saffron closed her eyes, the scar on her breast throbbing in memory of how venomous that blade could be. The solid sound of flesh against flesh followed by a painful grunt made her open her eyes, and her heart raced in terror at what she might see.

Guido was sprawled on the ground at Nico's feet, the knife lying inches away. Nico was breathing heavily, a small cut bleeding along his cheekbone. He wiped the blood away impatiently with the back of his hand before running his fingers through already disordered hair, his voice icy with anger as he said, 'Piero, I told you to watch Guido. And as for you, Guido, I warned you what would happen if . . .'

'Nico, look out!' Saffron shouted the warning as she saw Guido's fingers reach out for the knife, but Nico beat him to it, kicking it away with a savage oath, his eyes almost black as he bent to grasp Guido's shirt and dragged him to his feet.

'I should beat you to a pulp!'

'It wasn't Guido's fault,' Olivia objected, erupting on to the scene. 'She was taunting him, encouraging him . . .'

'I wasn't! She's lying!' The words formed themselves in Saffron's mind but refused to leave her tongue. The world became a whirling black vortex, devouring her in its midst, obliterating the nightmare engulfing her.

CHAPTER EIGHT

SAFFRON was lying on the narrow bed in her room. Darkness had fallen and she could see the moon through the uncurtained window. She got up, and everything that had happened came rushing back. She started to shake, swallowing hard on the sickness rising up inside her and feeling the pain of her bruised throat. And it was not only her throat that had suffered; there were bruises on her arms, and her blouse hung in shreds round her.

Dear God! She shuddered to think how close she had come to being raped. If Nico hadn't come in when he had! Nico! Tears started to pour from her eyes. She huddled on the bed, knees drawn up under her chin, arms folded protectively around them, curling her body into the smallest, tightest ball possible. The brief knock which preceded the opening of the door had her tensing every muscle. She caught a glimpse of Nico's closed, grim face, the dark shadowing of hair in the opening of his shirt, and turned away, shivering with nausea, her feelings reflected in her eyes before she closed them too late to conceal her expression from the man standing in the doorway with a small bowl in one hand and a tube of cream in the other.

'Saffron.' He said her name as softly as though he were calling some timid woodland creature, his voice perfectly even and soothing as he approached the bed, talking to her all the time. 'It's perfectly all right,' he told her, 'I don't want to hurt you. I just want to look and make sure your wound hasn't opened up again. I'll put some cream on your bruises. See, it doesn't hurt, does it?' he asked quietly, as she allowed him to take her arm and smooth some of the lotion on to it, her body tensed and wary.

'Saffron . . .'

Tears trembled on her lashes, her whole body shaking.

'Don't touch me.' She said it so quietly he had to bend his head to catch the anguished words. 'Don't come near me. I feel so dirty . . . so dirty . . .' She had started to rock from side to side, her eyes blank and unseeing. Nico reached for her, but she tensed against him, still trembling.

'Saffron, it's all right. He won't touch you again, I promise . . . It's all right. Come, let me take this blouse, and then you can wash—I'll bring you some water. You'll feel better.' He got up and walked to the door, but Saffron gave no indication of seeing or hearing him, her thin arms still locked round her taut body as she repeated over and over, 'So dirty . . . so dirty . . .'

When he came back she was still in the same position. Patiently, just as though she were a child, he unlocked her arms from her knees, straightening out the cramped limbs and removing her torn blouse. Although she flinched from the touch of his hands when he sponged her bruised flesh she didn't try to avoid him, and as his hand stroked softly over her skin some of the tension started to drain out of her. As though he sensed it Nico paused, his eyes searching her face before he said gently,

'You're all right, Saffron. Nothing happened. He didn't . . .'

'Rape me?' She shuddered deeply with the

words. 'But he was going to, and there wasn't anything I could do stop him. I could have died, and all I would have known was that.'

His voice and hands soothed her as he stroked her body and told her that it was over, holding her like a child in the comfort of his arms, only releasing her when he was sure that she had started to relax.

'I've brought you some water.' He gestured to the large bowl on the floor. 'I'll leave you to get washed, but I'll be back in half an hour with some supper.'

When he had gone Saffron got shakily to her feet, washing herself slowly like someone in the grip of a dream. The tattered remnants of her blouse provoked a fresh wave of remembered horror, but she quelled it and pulled on her other blouse. She was just buttoning it when Nico arrived with her supper.

She didn't want to eat it, but as though he sensed her refusal Nico said quietly, 'I'm not leaving until every bit of it has gone. Olivia tells me you've eaten nothing all day.'

'What's the point?' To her horror her voice shook, tears welling in her eyes.

'Come . . .' A spoonful of meat and pasta was held to her lips, and her mouth opened as obediently as a child's. Once she had taken a mouthful she realised how hungry she was. Nico had also brought her a mug of coffee, although when she tasted it she pulled a face over its strange flavour.

'Brandy,' Nico explained briefly. 'It will mitigate the shock and help you sleep.'

Sleep! How could she possibly sleep when every time she closed her eyes she saw Guido's face, felt his hands on her body? Her face worked. She put down the mug with exaggerated care.

'Nico . . .'

'I know, but it will pass.'

'How can you know?' she cried wildly. 'It hasn't happened to you—you haven't had to endure the . . . It was loathsome, hateful! I feel so . . . so defiled . . .'

'Saffron.' He said her name gently, taking hold of her arms and holding her so that she couldn't avoid the penetrating quality of his gaze. 'What happened was not your fault. If it was anyone's it was mine. I knew Guido wanted you; I told myself you were encouraging him, but I knew it wasn't true. No blame attaches to you. You must believe that.'

'How can I,' she cried painfully, 'when I know if he had raped me no one would have believed me? Every time anyone touches me it will seem like it's him . . . I can't . . .' She shuddered again, not seeing the way Nico's eyes darkened or the grim set of his mouth.

'Saffron, I . . .'

'Don't leave me alone tonight, Nico,' she begged half hysterically. 'Please don't leave me alone . . . I couldn't bear it, I. . . .'

'Hush . . . hush!' His arms were round her again, forcing her to relax.

'It's all right . . . Everything's fine. I'll stay. Come, lie down and try to sleep. I promise I'll be here if you need me.'

Strangely enough she did sleep, but only because Nico shared the narrow bed with her, holding her against the protective warmth of his body so that there was no way for Guido's image to impose itself on her mind.

There was barely room for them both on the small bed, and she woke some time during the night to find that she was curled against Nico's warmth, her head resting against his chest and her arms locked round his waist.

'Nico, are you awake?'

'Yes. Are you frightened?'

'Not while you're here, Guido . . .'

'Forget Guido,' he told her curtly. The old impatience was back in his voice, the sudden removal of his arms a shock of rejection. Pain shafted through her and all at once she started to shiver.

Nico's hands cupped her face, his, 'Saffron, don't,' releasing the tension inside her so that she cried as though she could never stop, silent, ceaseless tears that filled her eyes and soaked his shirt.

For several minutes he simply let her cry and Saffron was dimly conscious of the comforting warmth of his skin beneath her cheek, the stroke of his thumb as he brushed away the tears that were gradually easing.

She felt no fear in his embrace, no sense of panic when he gently traced the outline of her lips and then covered them with his own. She could feel the male warmth of him through the thin barrier of their clothes, her senses started to stir and she responded, stiffening suddenly as a mental image of Guido came between her and the man holding her in his arms. His fingers were lightly caressing the shape of her spine, but she was barely aware of his gently arousing touch. Sickness shivered inside her, the palms of her hands were moist with perspiration.

'Saffron.' There was regret and understanding in the way he spoke her name, slowly releasing her.

'No.'

From somewhere she found the courage to make the small, explosive protest, her hands going to Nico's shoulders, small fingers biting tensely into the solid muscle.

'No, don't leave me, Nico,' she whispered, adding pleadingly, 'Make love to me now.' When there was no response, she continued huskily, 'Don't you see? All I can remember is Guido; all I can feel, smell, hear . . .' She was starting to tense again, her eyes clinging despairingly to Nico's in the darkness. 'Please?' she begged, her mouth trembling. 'Please, I don't want that to be the only . . .'

'Saffron, you don't know what you're asking!'

The muted undertones carried a vehemence that sent anguish curling down to her toes, but she refused to acknowledge the pain of yet another rejection.

'Am I so undesirable?' she demanded brokenly, 'so sexless that you don't want me?' Her eyes searched his face again, and finding no response she added bitterly, 'Or is it that you can't bear to touch me now that Guido . . .'

She heard his stifled curse and then she was in his arms, held close to the hard contours of his body. 'Never say that again,' she heard him say grittily against her ear. 'No man worth his salt would let such a consideration stand in his way, and besides, Guido did not rape you. You are still a virgin, and it is for this reason . . .'

'Because I'm a virgin! Am I then to go a virgin to my death?' she asked him in a voice that trembled with resentment. 'Does my virginity somehow make me less desirable, less physically arousing? I want you, Nico,' she told him recklessly. 'I need you, I . . .'

'No, you don't,' came the grim rejoinder. 'You want someone to make love to you to banish the memory of Guido—I or any other, even half desirable male would do, and if I had the slightest atom of sense . . .' He looked down at her, cupping her face, his eyes hot and hungry. 'I want you, Saffron,' he groaned thickly, sliding his fingers into the short curls framing her face, 'and you're making it impossible for me to remember that I shouldn't have you.'

Saffron made no response. She knew instinctively that she needed the healing balm of Nico's lovemaking to destroy the memory of Guido's assault, and she knew just as instinctively that Nico would never physically abuse a woman, no matter what he might be or what his mission in life was.

When his mouth touched hers, she met his kiss with an eagerness that made him moan in protest, transforming his gentle possession of her lips into a white heat of mutual need that completely transcended anything Saffron had known or thought to know in the past.

His skin when she slid her fingers beneath his shirt felt hot, almost scorching her fingers, the pulsating fever of his body leaving no room for fear or second thoughts. In a gesture that was purely instinctive she moulded herself against him, glorying in the sudden tensing of his muscles, the tightly controlled shudder that ripped through him as he lifted his head and stared at her through the darkness.

'Oh, Saffron!' He said her name unevenly as though he was holding himself under tight control and unable to gauge how long that control would last out.

Saffron didn't want it to; she wanted his possession to be total and final, not tempered to accommodate her situation and inexperience. She wanted them to meet in equal need and desire; to lose herself completely in the bittersweet surrender of her body and forget all the whys and wherefores of what was happening.

'Saffron.'

This time there was resignation, and something else, that stirred a fever in her blood, in the way he said her name. Her lips parted willing beneath the hungry pressure of his; his kiss was totally devastating, and she quivered under the assault of his mouth a warm, insidious helplessness flooding through her, leaving her completely pliant and responsive.

His hands slid round her back, lifting her slightly so that she was lying against him, the warm sure touch of his fingers on her spine causing small explosions of pleasure inside her. Her own hands reached hungrily towards him, sliding inside his shirt, exploring the breadth of his shoulders and then trailing experimentally through the dark hair matting his chest. She heard his swiftly indrawn breath with a small gasp of pleasure that she actually had the power to move him, the tentative, almost feverish kisses she pressed against the warm, damp skin of his throat an indication of her growing urgency to experience everything there was to experience before it was too late. She was like a small child who had deliberately refused to open a single Christmas present before the appointed time, who suddenly foresaw the possibility of them all being removed, and now couldn't wait to unwrap the lot.

'Dear heaven, Saffron! Have you any idea of what you're doing to me?' Nico's piously unsteady demand, muttered into her ear, caused small convulsions of delight to course through her, and when he started to remove her blouse and bra she was achingly eager to be rid of them, to feel his hands against her bare flesh, to have those long skilled fingers appeasing the almost unbearable ache in her breasts, already swollen and acutely sensitive to his touch.

When he had removed her clothes he took her mouth in a long drugging kiss, not touching her at all, except to clamp her against him, his eyes so dark that they appeared black as he looked slowly down the length of her body and muttered hoarsely, '*Dio*, I must be out of my skull, but heaven help me, I want you. You're like an ache in the gut, a fever in the blood, Saffron, and you'll never know how many nights I've slept alone, wanting you like this in my arms, sweetly naked and wanting me.'

His words were like a magic incantation, banishing any lingering doubts about what she was doing, fanning her burning need to experience his possession before her life was extinguished.

'Undress me, Saffron.' The husky command was punctuated with ardent kisses as the warm male mouth slid moistly along the line of her throat, strong teeth nibbling softly at her earlobe, and tightening possessively on her shoulder when she complied with his request. There was something undeniably erotic about removing his clothes, about the new freedom to place random kisses against whichever part of his body she revealed as she unfastened and pulled off his shirt. Her fingers touched tentatively on the belt of his jeans and she paused. In the darkness she felt him tense, his husky, 'For heaven's sake don't stop now,' inciding her to struggle with the stiff leather until it suddenly gave way beneath her probing fingers, partially exposing the taut flatness of his belly, hard and arrowed with dark hair that felt crisp and alien to her touch.

All of a sudden he was breathing differently, the even rhythm broken, the sudden urgent possession of his hands as they caressed her breasts thrilling and just slightly frightening.

'What are you trying to do to me,' he moaned against her throat, 'drive me mad with frustration? Can't you tell how much I want to have you touch my body? Don't you know...' He tensed suddenly, all the passion dying out of his touch. 'Of course you don't,' he said in a flatly mocking voice. 'How could you? You're a virgin. I can't do this, Saffron,' he continued, tight-lipped. 'Don't...'

Here was her chance to back down, and she knew beyond any shadow of a doubt that she wasn't going to.

'Nico, please!' She bent her head and trailed soft kisses downwards over the dark shadowing of hair, feeling him tense and then jerk convulsively as he pulled her away.

'What's wrong?' she asked innocently. 'Don't you like me doing that?'

'You're not that naïve.' The words were bitten off and tight, every bone in his face hard beneath its tanned covering of skin. There was not enough room for him to hold her off on the narrow bed and despite the fabric of his jeans Saffron was aware of the urgent hardening of his thighs, the tautness of a body held on a very fine thread of control. She waited, breath held slightly in agonised apprehension, subduing hysterical laughter at the role reversal. Surely *she* should be the one hanging back, hesitant.

'What's the matter?'

He had sensed her laughter and she could feel him probing the darkness for an answer to his question.

'I never thought it would be so difficult to lose my virginity. Is that why you don't want me? Because of that?'

'Don't be bloody stupid!' Nico moved jerkily, pulling her ruthlessly against him so that she could not help but be aware of his arousal. 'Of course I damned well want you,' he muttered tight-lipped, 'but I want you as a woman, and I don't damned well know if I can exercise the self-restraint to initiate a virgin. Does that answer your question?' She felt him rake frustrated fingers through his hair, his groaned, 'Don't ask me to be more explicit or I might just show you,' shivering against her skin, provoking a reaction that committed her to a path from which there would be no turning back as she pressed herself against him, winding her arms round his neck, her lips teasing tiny kisses against his throat as she whispered encouragingly, 'Yes, please, Nico,' and felt, not without a tremor of reaction, the explosively expressive exhalation of breath fanning her hair before she was rolled over on to her back, the cool night air shafting across her skin, raising goosebumps as Nico got up.

For a moment she thought he was going to leave her, and tension coiled through her as she braced her body against rejection. But in the moonlight she saw that he was merely removing his jeans. He had his back to her, and she caught her breath, remembering how she had seen him after his swim in the river, and her eyes widened in startled appreciation of the total maleness of him, so that when he turned she was watching him with unashamed curiosity.

Instead of joining her on the bed, he dropped down at her side, his face hidden from her as he ran his hand gently along her body, and then again with greater urgency.

'Don't blame me if this doesn't turn out to be the way you've always imagined,' he warned her brutally. 'First times aren't necessarily good times.'

But it wasn't just her 'first time', it was going to be the only time, Saffron thought achingly, and then there was no room for thought as Nico's mouth followed the path taken by his hand, and she was trembling and arching against him, welcoming the bruising hardness of his body as he joined her on the bed, holding her against him while he plundered the moist sweetness of her mouth until she was dizzy and bemused by the sudden explosion of passion between them.

'Saffron!'

Her name jerked past his lips and she felt the sudden tensing of his body, as his mouth left the warm curve of her breast and possessed hers with the same hard determination with which he parted her thighs and slid heavily between them.

Panic flared and she fought to subdue it, but his hold on her wasn't relaxing, and neither was the pressure of his mouth. His hands had left breasts to hold and mould her hips as she arched feverishly against him, possessed by the same urgency she could feel emanating from him.

There was swift and agonising pain from which she recoiled instinctively, but the hard male hands refused to release her hips and she moaned in protest beneath the assault of his mouth, desire fleeing in the face of pain and panic.

It was over almost before it had begun, leaving her aching and restless, quivering with reaction to something she was not going to admit had in any way failed to live up to her expectations.

Unfortunately Nico didn't seem to share her reticence.

'Not quite the world-shattering experience you'd imagined?' he asked dryly. 'I did try to warn you. Never mind,' he mocked tersely, 'it will be different next time.'

'What next time?' she wanted to demand, but she was too tired, too defeated and depressed. Her eyes started to close and she neither knew nor cared that she was still lying naked in Nico's arms, the warmth of his body her only covering.

She woke during the night, escaping from the talons of a nightmare, Nico's voice reaching her out of the darkness, bringing her abruptly awake.

'It's all right,' he told her. 'It's only a nightmare. Guido isn't here. Or have I taken his place?'

She didn't pretend to misunderstand. Her body felt curiously light and fluid, and she flushed, remembering how earlier she had pleaded with him to make love to her. He had been right, the experience had not been what she had expected.

'You did warn me,' she admitted evenly.

'But you still expected to feel the earth move?' There was amusement in the words, firing fresh indignation as she grew accustomed to the dark and searched his face.

'Well, if it makes you feel any better, I've heard that it can, given the right circumstances and the right man. And anyway, it will never be as bad as that again, unless you make the mistake of choosing either a clumsy or inexperienced lover.'

'How would I do that?' she retorted bitterly. 'Olivia will never let me leave here alive—you know that.'

'And that was why you wanted me to make love to you?'

'Not entirely.' She had to be honest. 'It was so many things; Guido . . .' she shuddered. 'I couldn't bear only to be able to remember how I felt when he touched me, and . . .'

'Go on.' An iron inflexibility had entered his voice and warned her against refusing to answer.

'And I thought with you it would be different,' she told him candidly. 'I didn't realise . . .'

'That I'm only human?' he demanded wryly with a twisted smile. 'That I can only endure so much provocation without finding it physically impossible to draw back? Perhaps I ought to do something to get back on my pedestal, mm?'

For a moment she didn't realise what he meant, but when his fingers started to move seductively against her skin and her whole body trembled convulsively against him she realised, and tried to tense away. But Nico wouldn't let her. His skilled arousal of her body was something she had no defences against, and something that shocked and startled her after her earlier pain. Her body seemed to have no recollection of it, because it was responding to Nico as though it welcomed and accepted him as its lover. Her breasts peaked

urgently beneath his sensual stroking, hardening at
the first touch of his lips. Lips that teased and
tormented until she was reaching towards him, her
hands locking feverishly behind his neck, her
fingers curling into his hair, her whispered 'Nico,'
bringing the response she ached for and the warm
possession of his mouth against the aroused centre
of her breast.

And he didn't stop there. This time, without the
heated urgency of before, his hands and mouth
stroked lingeringly across her body, making her
tremble when they caressed the vulnerability of her
flat stomach and moved lower to the slender curve
of her thighs, causing a frenetic response to his
lovemaking that had her pressing mutely pleading
kisses against his own body, touching it as she had
not dared touch it before, letting him guide and
instruct her until she was soft and pliant in his
arms, and this time his possession was accomplished without pain or withdrawal as she was
coaxed gently into relaxing until she was free to
experience the pleasure he was giving her, his name
muffled beneath his mouth as he carried her
upwards with him to gaze spellbound and dazzled
at the full glory of the sun before she sank into
black velvet darkness, emotional tears leaving
damp tracks against Nico's skin.

When at last she was capable of speech, and
Nico's heartbeat had stopped sounding like
thunder and resumed a normal reassuring thud,
she pressed a shy kiss against his throat and
murmured a hesitant, 'Thank you.'

She couldn't see his face, but there was a good
deal of wryness in the way he said, 'It's more usual
for the man to do the thanking, especially after an
experience like that . . .'

Saffron didn't know what he meant and felt too shy and tired to ask, but she would ask him in the morning, she promised herself as her eyes closed, and sleep washed over her.

Saffron opened her eyes. Something was different. She frowned, trying to remember what it was, and then realisation came flooding over her. She was alone in the bed, but still naked beneath the cover that Nico had obviously tucked round her before leaving.

Common sense told her that she ought to feel shame, or at the very least regret, for what had happened, but she couldn't. What she did feel was an intense bubbling sensation of happiness, and a warm rippling pleasure in her own body. She stretched luxuriously, aware of herself in a way she had never been until Nico taught her. Nico. Warmth filled her. His lovemaking had been everything she had ever dreamed of, but where was he?

An alien sound reached her from outside, and she ran to the window, just in time to see a helicopter circling the farmhouse. Hope that she had suppressed for so long flared up inside her. Did that mean that they were actually looking for her? Surely a helicopter in these remote parts must mean something?

Tense and excited, she started to dress. Downstairs she could hear sounds of activity. Nico would be down there. He too would have seen the helicopter, but with very different emotions. For the first time she faced the sobering thought that they were on opposite sides; that her freedom meant he had failed, and Olivia had made it plain what happened to failures. A terrible fear engulfed her, but she forced it away. She felt nothing for Nico as a person, nothing at all. Heavens, if it hadn't been for her situation she would never have dreamed of letting him so much as kiss her, never mind . . .

The door opened and he came in, stern and unsmiling.

'Good, you're dressed.' He spoke in clipped accents. 'We're leaving.'

'Because of the helicopter?' she asked, greatly daring.

'So you saw it? Yes. Olivia has just reminded me that it was my idea that we stay here. She isn't feeling very kindly towards you this morning,' Nico added dryly, watching the colour run up under her skin with detached interest. 'So we're back to being the aloof Miss Wykeham now that you realise that you haven't been completely forgotten by the outside world? Last night was just an aberration, something which is to be forgotten and swept under the carpet, is that it?' His mouth twisted. 'Very well then, so be it.'

Something not unlike regret shafted through her; a sense of having failed him in some way, which was ridiculous in all the circumstances, and yet as she brushed past him in the open doorway, her arm moving lightly against the bare skin of his, sensations not unlike those she had experienced during the night came rushing over her and for one weak moment she wanted to cling to him and beg him to leave, now, while there was still time. She looked up at him, tears blurring her sight, her throat aching with the pain of knowing that her rescue must mean his downfall, but his expression warned her against voicing her feelings, so she went downstairs to face Olivia's bitter hatred and the glowering menace from Guido as he watched by the window.

The plan was that they left immediately after they had eaten. Saffron gathered from what was being said that they had another safe house they had prepared before they kidnapped her, and it was to this that they were going to take her now.

'I told you we had stayed here too long,' Olivia snarled at Nico. 'I warned you that her father was playing with us, but oh no, you knew best, or was it simply that you wanted more time to bed her? I hope you enjoyed it,' she said pithily, 'because when Rome hears . . .'

'Rome will hear nothing until I say so,' Nico told her curtly. 'Piero, go outside and help Guido with the Land Rover—something seems to be wrong, he's still trying to start it.'

He was, and for several minutes the sounds continued, until Piero reappeared, grim and angry.

'It won't start,' he announced. 'Heaven knows what's wrong with it. Fuel's getting through all right, but the damn thing peters out almost as soon as it's fired.'

'Well then, start the other one,' Nico commanded him testily—and yet in spite of his outward manner, Saffron had the impression that he was not really concerned whether they got away or not, strange though it seemed.

Piero shrugged, 'Same thing.' He frowned suddenly, then turned and opened the canister used to store sugar. 'How much was in here last night?' he asked Olivia.

Puzzled, Saffron saw the other girl's eyes widen as she stared at the plastic canister.

'Your little girl-friend's put sugar in the petrol!'

Piero informed Nico savagely. 'That's why the damned thing won't start!'

'You mean we're trapped here?' Olivia looked bitter. 'When they come back, we'll be caught like rats in a trap!'

'If they come back,' Nico pointed out. 'We don't know for sure . . .'

'Oh no, we don't know for sure, but we can make a pretty educated guess. It's the police all right, and they won't be coming back unarmed. Still, we've still got the girl. Daddy isn't going to like having her pumped full of holes in front of him, which is what we'll do unless he hands over the money and gives us a guaranteed free passage out of the country.'

Cornered rats were dangerous, Saffron thought with a sinking heart. Neither Piero nor Nico had argued with Olivia, and Saffron had no doubt at all that the Italian girl would do exactly what she had said if the need arose. But they were mistaken about the sugar. She hadn't touched it!

'Lock her upstairs for now,' Nico told Olivia tersely. He moved, and for the first time Saffron realised that he was carrying a gun—not like those held by the others, but a snub-nosed, wicked-looking revolver type gun. A fine film of sweat covered her body. Dear heaven, if this was being rescued she almost preferred imprisonment!

'No. She stays down here, where we can watch her,' Olivia argued. 'We keep her with us—they'll be that much more careful about how they fire their guns. How long do you think it will be before they get here?'

She was frightened, even Saffron could see that; and she couldn't help noticing how all three of them, even Guido, now turned to Nico for advice and instructions.

'It all depends how far they have to come. Say two hours—that is if they've guessed that we're here.' He glanced at his watch. 'We might as well start getting ready now. Olivia, take Saffron with you and bring in all the food stores—we don't know how long we're likely to be penned up in here. Guido, Piero, bring in the extra rounds of ammunition.'

'Aren't you going to warn Rome?' Olivia wetted dry lips and looked at him.

'What's the point? They couldn't send reinforcements in time. No, we're in this on our own.'

Strangely Nico seemed almost to be enjoying the situation, Saffron noted, while the other three were plainly unnerved by it. They were all bullies at heart, she realised with sudden awareness. Everything was fine while they were doing the bullying, but let someone bigger come along and threaten them and it was a far different story.

In the event Nico was out by half an hour. Almost exactly one and a half hours after Saffron had first seen it, the helicopter returned, circling the farmhouse before dropping down to land out of sight by the river.

'Damn, they're out of range!' Piero snarled, leaving the window he had been guarding. 'What do you think they'll do? Rush us, or wait it out?'

'Depends.' Nico seemed remarkably unaffected.

'On what?' Olivia demanded in a shrill voice.

'On whether it's the Italians, or whether Sir Richard Wykeham has been able to convince the British Government that as a British citizen his daughter has a right to expect the protection of their own troops.'

Olivia went white. 'The S.A.S.?' she demanded huskily. 'But the Italian authorities would never agree!'

'After the bloodbath of Moreau? I should think they'd be grateful to anyone who took the whole potentially embarrassing situation out of their hands. After all, that's one of the organisation's aims, isn't it? To bring down and disgrace the government? Total anarchy?'

Puzzled, Saffron wondered if Nico realised that he was increasing his companions' fears rather than allaying them. It was almost as though he knew how terrified they were at the thought of facing the S.A.S. and was deliberately playing on it, but she must be imagining things, surely?

'Nico, down by the olive grove . . . look!'

Guido's tense words banished all thoughts of why Nico had behaved as he had from Saffron's mind, and like the others her total concentration was on the shadowy figures moving through the olive grove. What would they do?' she wondered dry-mouthed. The Italian method seemed to be to rush the building, and everyone inside, but the British were renowned for their use of diplomacy before force.

In the event it proved to be the latter. A man wearing camouflage clothing approached the farmhouse, carrying a loudhailer, flanked on either side by others carrying machine-guns.

He spoke through it in Italian, requesting Saffron's release. Guido's response was to fire off a round of ammunition. Saffron saw the men flatten themselves to the ground and the next moment Nico was pushing her down on to the floor herself.

'Keep down,' he mouthed curtly, ducking his

own head as machine-gun fire ricocheted through the building.

The following hours were a time Saffron could never remember clearly afterwards. She was conscious of fear, and almost unbearable heat and tension in the small room. Sporadic bursts of gunfire interspersed with reminders that they could never escape the building alive seemed to be the answer from the soldiers outside to her captor's refusal to let her go.

How long it lasted Saffron wasn't sure. Time seemed to drag by on leaden feet, and fear cramped through her stomach as she thought how close freedom was and yet how far away. Death was as near as the gun in Olivia's hand, the knife at Guido's belt, and neither would hesitate for one moment, she knew that.

Nico was lying full length on the floor beside her, guarding one of the windows, when she tried to crawl away, hoping somehow to escape upstairs without being seen and perhaps from there draw the attention of her rescuers, his fingers clamped round her wrist. Holding her did not seem to deflect from his aim, and she winced as she saw him level the gun and fire.

'You will never take us alive!' Olivia screamed at one point when they had been subjected to another plea to give themselves up. 'Nor will you get the girl back. We will kill her first!'

After that there seemed to be a lull outside. Guido went upstairs to check on any movement at the back of the farmhouse, but no sooner had he gone than another burst of firing from outside diverted the others' attention to their attackers.

Saffron was facing the stairs, lying on her stomach, her muscles cramped in protest, but too

terrified of being hit by a stray bullet to move, and
so she was the first to see the four figures emerging
from upstairs, guns at the ready, their camouflage
distinctively reassuring.

Afterwards she could not have said what
prompted her, but instead of keeping quiet, she
tugged instinctively on Nico's arm. His head
swung round, and at the same moment Olivia
screamed, 'Nico—the girl, kill her now!' Saffron
saw her raise her gun. Nico sat up, dragging
Saffron with him, at the precise moment when the
door was forced open.

Saffron heard his muttered, 'The door—run,
quickly!' in a daze, and obeyed instinctively, seeing
too late, as she stood up, the purpose in Olivia's
eyes. Nico moved, thrusting himself between her
body and the gun; there was a loud explosion, the
force of it seeming to carry her to the door, then
camouflaged men caught her as she fell, unaware
of the name falling achingly from her lips as they
reassured themselves that she was unhurt before
advancing into the mêlée inside the room.

'Nico . . . Nico . . .' She was still sobbing his
name, as familiar arms came round her in
unfamiliar clothing, her father's face haggard as he
looked down into hers.

'Oh, my poor baby!' He held her to him,
strangely unfamiliar in the uniform he was
wearing, older and graver than she remembered,
and then another man, obviously an officer, was
suggesting discreetly that they left the men to get
on with the job they had come to do, indicating a
waiting Land Rover. As her father helped her into
it, Saffron looked back over her shoulder. Gunfire
echoed from the farmhouse, now enveloped in
dense smoke.

'They've got orders to take them alive,' her father told her grimly, plainly not happy with the orders, 'but fortunately they'll stand trial in Italy, which will mean they'll get much harsher sentences—life imprisonment at the very least.'

Life imprisonment! Saffron thought of Nico confined to a cell and something twisted inside her. He had saved her, she thought numbly, surely that must mean something. She turned to her father, wanting to tell him so, but he silenced her unsteadily and hugging her. 'Oh, my poor darling girl! I can't wait to get you home. We'll go away somewhere together, have a proper holiday, put all this behind us.'

Numbly Saffron agreed, refusing to admit that some aspects of her imprisonment at least would not be easy to forget. She was free and safe, and she must concentrate on that and try to forget . . . everything else.

CHAPTER NINE

NATURALLY enough Saffron's capture and subsequent rescue caused something of a nine-day wonder in the press, when the news became public. Columnists who had dismissed her as gossip column fodder now hounded her for interviews, until it became almost impossible for her to set a foot outside her father's apartment.

Her new relationship with her father was an unexpected bonus she had not anticipated, and his tender care and concern for her touched her deeply. He was planning to take her away on holiday as soon as pressure of business allowed. So far they had not discussed her ordeal—she had expressed a wish not to do so, and he had acquiesced, although warning her that she simply could not bury the whole incident out of sight.

Every day she scoured the press for some mention of her kidnappers; the role of the S.A.S. in her rescue was being kept very low-key; the only reason they had been involved was because her father's company was engaged in the production of a new highly technical weapon, and it had been feared that somehow this had been leaked to her kidnappers, the Government had stepped in, or so her father had told her.

However, no matter how carefully she scrutinised the press Saffron saw nothing about the raid on the farmhouse or its result. She told herself that it was natural that she should be curious about the fate of her kidnappers, but it was only one of them

who occupied so many of her thoughts—Nico.
Had he escaped, or had he been taken captive? She
told herself that she should feel pleasure in the
possibility of his capture, that her own humiliation
had been avenged, but all she could feel was a dull
aching pain.

A month after her rescue her father took her to
the Caribbean, where they spent an idyllic
fortnight lying on pale silver sands beneath deeply
azure skies—or at least it should have been idyllic.
Saffron didn't find it so. She was still tense and on
edge, jumping at the lightest footfall, too edgy to
appreciate the lighthearted conversation and
company of the other young people at the hotel.

'When we get back I'm going to concentrate
more on my job,' she told her father firmly one
morning. 'What we're doing now is just the tip of
the iceberg.'

'Just as long as you don't spend all our profits
on these welfare schemes,' her father teased in
response. He had been treating her as though she
were made of glass and he was terrified she was
going to break into a thousand shimmering pieces.

In an effort to reassure him she talked over her
plans with him on the flight home. It was a long
one, eight hours, and Saffron woke up just before
the false dawn cramped and stiff, to hear the pilot
announcing over the tannoy that they were having
to put down at the nearest airport.

'Slight engine trouble—nothing serious,' he
reassured his passengers.

'Better safe than sorry,' a smiling stewardess
commented to Saffron as she came to check that
seat-belts were all fastened. 'They've got another
plane standing by, so you won't be delayed for too
long.' She gave Saffron's father an especially

charming smile. Her father was still a very
attractive man, Saffron found herself realising with
a small start, wondering if he had ever thought of
remarrying, having other children. She realised
with a stab of shame that she knew little or
nothing of her father's hopes and dreams; and
worse still, that she hadn't wanted to know,
treating him merely as a distant provider whose
presence could otherwise be ignored. From now
on, though, all that was going to change. She
squeezed his hand as they started to descend,
listening to him talk to the stewardess.

'Where are we putting down?' she asked the girl
incuriously as she headed back to her own seat in
the rear of the aircraft.

'Rome,' the other girl told her, 'but there won't
be time for any sightseeing, if that's what you're
thinking!'

Rome! The pressure of her father's fingers
increased slightly, his eyes compassionate and
understanding as they met hers. Poor Daddy, in a
way it was worse for him than it was for her. So
far she had told him nothing about her ordeal;
nothing about Nico.

As the stewardess had said, they were not
delayed at all at the airport. A fresh plane was
standing by, but as they hurried to their departure
gate Saffron's attention was caught by the
headlines on a newspaper.

'Kidnap gang to be brought to early trial,' they
screamed. 'English Lord's daughter to stand as
witness.' There was more which she barely had
time to see, something about her being the only
one of their victims ever to be found alive, but
Saffron couldn't read it all because her father was
hurrying her past, his face pale and drawn.

'You never told me,' she accused when they were settled in their new plane.

'I didn't want to upset you. You don't have to appear at the trial if you don't want to, in fact I told Dom . . .'

'Dom?'

'Dom Hunter,' her father explained. 'His godfather and I were partners . . . I don't think you've ever met him. He's several years older than you, thirty odd.'

'No, I haven't,' Saffron agreed shortly. 'But what does he have to do with the trial?'

'Nothing, except he's a brilliant lawyer, and we were discussing the possibility of you having to appear before we came away. He said I should warn you, but rightly or wrongly I wanted you to have this break free from anything like that hanging over you. In fact, as I told Dom, I don't want you to appear . . .'

'But if I don't they won't be able to convict the gang, will they?' Saffron asked slowly, remembering what she had read.

'I don't believe so,' her father agreed gravely, shaking his head. 'You're the only witness, for want of a better word, but I don't want you exposed to any more danger or upset.'

'Danger? You mean from other members of the gang?'

'I believe most of them are now in custody,' her father told her. 'From what they learned from your kidnappers the police were able to trace the others.'

Her father seemed to know a surprising amount about the whole thing; far more than he had indicated to her.

'I asked to be kept informed,' he told her,

guessing her thoughts. 'And of course the Italian authorities had a considerable amount of help from our people, although it's all very much a diplomatic secret.'

'I suppose I'm fortunate in having a father with secrets the Government want to keep secret,' Saffron replied soberly. 'Otherwise . . .'

'Don't think about it,' her father suggested softly. 'Perhaps Dom's right and appearing in court will prove a cartharsis for you. You've never talked to me about what happened.'

'But you've obviously talked a good deal to Dom,' Saffron said bitterly, biting her lip as she saw his unhappy expression. 'I'm sorry, Daddy,' she apologised instantly, 'that wasn't fair of me.'

'I've been worried about you,' he said simply. 'For all the difference in our age, Dom is a good friend and one whose judgment I value.'

The subject wasn't mentioned again until they reached home, where Saffron found a large official-looking envelope waiting for her.

As she had anticipated, it turned out to be from the Italian authorities. She took it up to her room with her, and wisely her father let her go without speaking. Once there she curled up in the rocking chair she had had from childhood, now painted a soft peach to tone with the sophistication of her room.

Strange to think how at the beginning of her captivity she would have relished this moment, enjoyed the thought of Nico being sent to prison, deprived of his freedom as she had been deprived of hers. But now . . .

As she sat staring into space, events and emotions which had previously been alien and bewildering clicked into space and she stared sightlessly down at the letter as the truth struck her with the force of a blow.

She loved Nico! That was why she had not been able to enjoy her holiday; had spent so many nights lying awake, so many days trying to combat the deep ache inside her. What she had mistakenly thought of as merely sexual desire, a need to experiment before her life was cut short, had in reality been her body's way of urging her towards the truth. Had she merely wanted to experiment she would have turned equally easily to Guido or Piero, surely, but instead she had wanted Nico and only Nico.

She had been halfway to falling in love with him when she saw him on the beach, and the hothouse atmosphere of the farmhouse had forced that love into early and heady flowering.

Suddenly she knew what she must do. It wouldn't be easy, and would undoubtedly shock and hurt her father, but she loved Nico and she was prepared to fight for him no matter what he had done in the past. Surely when she told the authorities how he had saved her life in those desperate minutes, when he had pushed her out of the way of Olivia's gun, they would judge him less harshly? She knew he hadn't been involved in those other kidnappings. But she didn't know what he had been doing, she reminded herself; she didn't even know how he felt about her. But that didn't matter. She wanted to save him with the same intensity with which she had once wanted to see him punished.

If her father found her determination to attend the trial strange, he made no comment about it. Saffron wrote back to the Italian authorities, telling them that she would stand as a witness. She had decided to make her plea for Nico from the witness box; that way it would have more authority, more shock value.

She wasn't entirely stupid, though; she could well imagine the field day the press would have, insinuating that somehow Nico had warped her judgment; and all the past gossip about her would be resurrected, but she no longer cared. Nico knew the truth.

The trial was a month away and there wasn't a day when she didn't think about Nico, nor a night when she didn't dream his arms were round her and she would wake up with her head pillowed against his chest, his body inflaming hers with its proximity.

The beautician who normally looked after her at her favourite beauty salon had been appalled by the state of her nails and skin. The destruction of her hair-style she had been able to correct by opting for a shorter, softer look than she had worn previously. He preferred it, her father had told her, and Saffron couldn't deny that it was softly and flatteringly feminine.

For the court hearing, which had been brought forward because the authorities were worried that any stray members of the gang not rounded up might try and break their friends free, Saffron had chosen a silk outfit in a rich golden yellow that echoed her name and brought out the golden lights in her auburn hair and tawny eyes. It made her look older, or was it simply that she had matured? Sir Richard told her that she looked enchanting, but privately he thought she looked heartbreakingly fragile and vulnerable, and he wished he knew what brought the shadows to her eyes and the droop to her mouth, but he was too wise and understanding to probe; their new relationship too precious to withstand any rough handling.

He had wanted to go to Italy with her, but Saffron had refused, and anyway, a sudden business trip to New York the week the trial started meant that he could not have accompanied her.

The weekend before she was due to leave he returned home early on the Friday night. Saffron had been busy packing—the saffron suit and the other clothes she would need for the first few days of the trial when she would be giving evidence. Her father came up to her room looking tired and anxious.

'I know you're going to object to this,' he began without preamble, 'but I've arranged for someone to go to Rome with you.'

'Not the inestimable Dom?' Saffron said sarcastically. She was a little tired of her father's constant enthusiastic references to his friend, but he ignored her rude comment and shook his head.

'No, one of the men who stormed the farmhouse. He's going to give evidence as well.'

Evidence which might convict Nico! Saffron tensed. This was something she hadn't planned for. This man her father was referring to must be one of the S.A.S. men who had rescued her.

If he was she didn't recognise him, but then she could remember very little about that day. He was both pleasant and polite as he took his seat beside her, and became engrossed in a biography of Winston Churchill once they were airborne.

She hadn't realised how tense she was until the flight was nearly over, when he said quietly to her, 'It must be hard for you to do this . . . especially when you lived so closely with them. It's one of the things we learn during training,' he added informatively. 'It goes one of two ways—either a deep and abiding hatred develops in the victim, or an intense sense of dependency.'

He was watching her, and despite his politeness Saffron sensed that he was wondering which applied to her. He would know soon enough, she thought, folding her lips into a tight line. It was true, she was dependent on Nico. Without him life would hold no real meaning, and yet she knew that it was more than likely that he didn't return her feelings. But if she could get him freed, if her father could be persuaded to help, surely then Nico would need her? She moved restlessly in her seat. Was that what she wanted? Cowed gratitude, dependence because there was nothing else for him? Did she really want him reduced to that? Hadn't she loved him because he was proud and independent? Would he really want his freedom at such a price, or would any feelings he might have for her turn to hatred and contempt? Backwards and forwards she argued with herself during the short flight, and was no nearer coming to any conclusion when it was over. All she did know was that she couldn't allow Nico to go to prison without at least trying to save him; what happened or didn't happen after that must be up to him.

With the armed guard that met them at the airport and surrounded her hotel came the realisation of how seriously the authorities were taking the trial and how little chance she had of actually helping Nico. The Italian Government was out for blood, and with Saffron's help they intended to get it, she realised that on the first day of the trial, when she was invited to take the witness stand and tell the jury how she had come to be kidnapped.

In the stand she could see Olivia, staring sullenly at her; Guido and Piero at her side, and behind them others whom she did not recognise, but Nico's face was not among them. Fear and panic began to build up inside her. Where was he?

The questions continued to come, and she forced herself to answer them as best she could, always without implicating Nico, her tension growing second by second as she searched the courtroom for him. Had he escaped? There had been nothing in the papers.

At one point where she was forced to disclose how Guido had attacked her, the room started to spin hazily round her and her voice became husky and strained. The judge was kind and fatherly. A glass of watered wine was brought to her and she was offered a chair.

'And at this point you were saved by another member of the gang?' the judge questioned, reading from the statement Saffron had given just after she was rescued. 'This man . . . is he here with the others?'

Someone walked over to the judge and whispered something in his ear. He nodded slowly. 'Ah yes,' he smiled at Saffron, 'I was forgetting—the man in question was shot during the fighting when you were rescued and is now beyond human justice.'

The courtroom swayed and tilted, spinning crazily round her. Nico was dead . . . dead . . . Sound encroached and receded in heavy waves; someone at the back of the courtroom was shouting; the man who had travelled with her on the plane was running towards her, a gun in his hand. Suddenly violence erupted in the small courtroom. Someone screamed and Saffron was pushed to the floor, just as a knife whistled past her ear. Shots rang out, and when at last Saffron raised her head, all she could see was Guido's sprawled, motionless body, and Olivia's contorted bitter face.

Just for a moment the scene changed and it was Nico's body lying where Guido was; Nico's arms outflung, body devoid of life, and the searing intensity of her loss outweighed every other emotion.

Over her head she heard her S.A.S. guard curse; and then he was turning to her, asking if she was all right. 'Dom warned me to expect something like this,' he muttered, but the remark had no meaning for Saffron. Nico was dead.

But she couldn't leave it there. After what had happened to her there was no question of her giving further evidence, but she refused to leave the court until she had learned the full circumstances surrounding Nico's death.

There was pity and compassion in her guard's eyes, when she told him that he would have to carry her out bodily and that she wasn't leaving until she knew everything. There was another emotion she couldn't give a name to as well, an almost guilty look.

She saw it again when she eventually managed to talk to one of the officials, a dapper, grim-faced Italian who spoke perfect English and who apologised profusely for what had so nearly happened. '*Bastardi!* These animals are not fit to live,' he said bitterly. 'They want to tear down the very fabric of civilisation, even to the extent of murdering His Holiness. They do not deserve to live.'

A pleading glance at her guard had him interrupting the man's monologue to ask the questions Saffron found she could not now frame.

'Miss Wykeham is concerned about the man Nico. He was shot and killed, I believe, during her rescue.'

Was it her imagination or did some silent message pass between the two men?

After the merest hesitation, the Italian agreed, 'Yes, that is so.'

'He died at the farmhouse?' Something was driving her to learn the truth, no matter how painful. She had to know—she must know how Nico had died.

'Yes. He was shot by one of your rescuers——'

'One of his own gang.'

The two explanations came simultaneously, and a frown touched Saffron's forehead, but before she could query the apparent discrepancy in their explanations the Italian apologised smoothly, 'Yes, of course, you are right—I am mistaken, he was shot by one of your rescuers.'

Nico dead! She could not take it in. He had been so magnificently alive, so inviolate and armoured in his strength of will. Hysterical sobs shook her body. Her S.A.S. guard looked uncomfortable, as did the Italian.

'*Signorina*, please . . .'

'What happened to his body?'

Silence.

'He . . . he has been buried.'

'And his grave?'

'Unmarked, as befits such a criminal,' the Italian told her, and it seemed to be the final blow. Nico was gone as though he had never been and there wasn't even a grave to mark his time on earth.

The S.A.S. man seemed anxious to get her away from the court, and she had the distinct impression that he was anxious for her not to ask any more questions, almost as though something were being hidden from her, but what?

Her father was waiting for her when their plane touched down at Heathrow, but when he saw her remote, shuttered face, and the way she moved, slowly and painfully as though she were about to shatter into a million tiny fragments, he made no move to touch her. Without giving her the opportunity to protest he arranged for them to go down to Surrey. Saffron couldn't remember the last time they had spent time together in the country, but although she tried to force herself to respond to her father's mood, it was impossible.

Nico haunted her. Only in losing him did she realise the intensity of her love for him; so much so that every conscious minute without him was a physical pain, and worse than everything else, the fact that she didn't know where his body lay; that she couldn't go there and find some comfort in being there.

She confided as much in her father, hoping that he might have enough influence to discover where Nico was buried, but to her dismay he seemed strangely reluctant to help. 'It will only make it harder for you,' was his explanation, but Saffron had a peculiar conviction that this was not his real reason, and once again the thought floated elusively through her mind that she was not being told the full truth. But what more could there be?

Even her desperate wish that she might have conceived Nico's child was denied her. Her father urged her to try and take up the threads of life again, but she felt no urge to do so. Four days after they had arrived at the house, to please her father, she agreed to his suggestion that they lunch out. He drove them himself to a small pub, well patronised by locals, and ordered a meal for them both.

The pâté which was served with mouthwatering homemade bread was coarse-grained and appetising, but Saffron had barely taken a mouthful when she saw a man standing up at the far end of the room, dark hair curling into his collar, his movements fluid and sure. She only had the merest glimpse of a back view of him, but it was enough to drive the colour from her face, Nico's name falling achingly from her lips. Her father's reactions were swift, as he moved to shield Saffron's pale face and shaking body from the other diners.

'It couldn't have been Nico, Saffron,' he told her quietly, but there was a look in his eyes Saffron found it hard to analyse, compounded of guilt and anger. When he was sure she had fully recovered he told her that he had just remembered a phone call he should have made before leaving the house.

Watching him disappear towards the telephone, Saffron tried to pull herself together. Her father seemed to be gone for a long time, and when he returned he looked thoughtful and preoccupied.

They left the pub almost immediately, but it wasn't until they were back at the house that he said softly, 'I know you've already given me the basics of what happened when you were held prisoner—I know how you feel about Nico, but you've kept so much to yourself, Saffron. Would it help to talk about it?'

'Oh, Daddy!' She flung herself into his arms, her fragile composure cracking completely, as she sobbed out her story and he listened in silence.

When she came to the end he looked very grave, and very much older. 'My poor darling girl,' he said sadly, 'what can I say? You talk of love for this man, are you sure it isn't simply infatuation—intensified by the fact that you know he's unattainable? Even if he had survived . . .'

'Would he have wanted me?' she asked soberly. 'Daddy, I don't know. I only know that I love him, and without him life is simply existence.' Her fingers rested lightly on her stomach, and he followed the gesture before saying softly, 'You were lovers, weren't you?'

She nodded, slow tears spilling down her cheeks.

'Yes, and believe it not, he was the first. He didn't want to, but I insisted, and I'm glad,' she cried desperately. 'At least I've had that. And don't tell me that I'm young and there'll be someone else; there never will—not someone like Nico.'

'Oh, my poor girl! What can I say? That time heals? It does, you know. When I first lost your mother . . .' He sighed, and seem to age even more. 'Saffron, I've misjudged you, and worse . . .'

'Because you didn't think I was capable of such love?' she asked sadly. 'Or perhaps because I said Nico was the first? I can't blame you, Daddy, my press hasn't been good.'

'What can I say? You're too old to be fed platitudes, and too young to accept that eventually they prove to be correct.'

But nevertheless Saffron knew he watched her with growing sadness when they returned to London. She worked doggedly in the office, and even enrolled on a course for secretarial work, but work was the only means of exhausting herself enough to sleep at night, and she needed her sleep because in her dreams Nico was always there, always loving, always warm and alive.

Christmas came and went. Her hair had started to grow long again. She was too thin, brittle and fragile as glass. The pain was getting worse, not better.

In the New Year her father had to go to New York again. The week before his trip he seemed on edge and unusually nervous. When Saffron tackled him with it, he said that it was because he didn't like the thought of leaving her alone. 'I've asked Dom to call round and see that everything's okay,' he told her, avoiding her eyes. 'He's in Sweden at the moment on business, but he'll be back next week. He's got a key to the penthouse.'

They were back in London and Saffron wanted to tell him that she didn't need keeping an eye on as though she were a witless child, but he looked so grave and careworn that she didn't have the heart.

'Saffron, I . . .' he began when she didn't demur, breaking off to say unevenly, 'May heaven forgive me for what I've done to you, because I can't forgive myself. If I'd known . . .'

Thinking he was referring to the fact that but for having a wealthy father she would never have been kidnapped, never have met Nico, she said softly,

'Daddy, there's nothing to forgive, just the opposite. What happened with Nico is more precious to me than anything else in life, and even though I'll never see him or touch him again my life is richer because of what happened. Perhaps you're right and it's better this way; at least I can pretend that he might have felt something for me . . .'

'Of course he did,' her father interrupted explosively. 'Saffron, I . . .'

Knowing that he was trying to ease her pain, she managed a shaky laugh. 'What do you mean, "of course he did"—why should he? Because I'm your daughter?' she teased.

He left the following afternoon. Saffron drove him to the airport, driving the heavy Rolls with skill. Afterwards instead of returning to the penthouse she drove to the office, engrossing herself in work, until she was so tired that she could have slept at her desk.

For several days she was at work by eight in the morning, not leaving until eight at night, when she returned to the penthouse, too exhausted even to eat, but gradually her body adapted to the punishing pace, and sleep became more elusive.

'Saffron, you can't go on like this,' her boss told her one morning when he arrived to find her already seated at her desk, huge circles beneath her eyes. 'Take a few days off—and that's an order! You're no use to me working like a zombie the way you are at the moment.'

Acknowledging the truth of his comment, Saffron gave in. The penthouse seemed stark and sterile without her father, and on impulse she decided to go down to Surrey.

Snow started to fall as she left London, tiny fluttering flakes, so vulnerable and yet so tenacious, like her love for Nico. It had grown without her being aware of it, until it was too late. Too late—the saddest words in any language, she thought drearily as she manoeuvred the heavy car through the traffic.

It was late when she reached the house, and as she unlocked the door, she made a mental note to ring her father. He would be worried if he phoned the penthouse and she wasn't there. The drive had made her tired; tired enough to be able to sleep almost immediately she slipped into bed, into the dreams where Nico was always with her.

CHAPTER TEN

SAFFRON woke up to discover that a thick cover of snow masked the gardens and surrounding countryside. Because the house wasn't used regularly her father normally only employed help on a temporary basis, but someone came in every week to check that everything was in order and it was no problem for Saffron to switch on the central heating.

While the house was heating up she decided to telephone her father, but to her dismay when she lifted the receiver it was to discover that the line was dead. The nearest phone box was three miles away at a crossroads. She had always wondered who had sited it there, miles away from anywhere. She shrugged, deciding that she would ring the exchange from the callbox on her way back from the village where she would have to go to buy food.

The snow was deeper than she had first thought; the Rolls was heavy despite the power-assisted steering, and her arms were aching by the time she reached the village.

There was only one general food store plus a butcher's, but Saffron managed to buy everything she wanted. It started snowing again as she drove back to the house. Just as she came up to the crossroads, a car turned the corner too fast, accelerating wildly towards her down the steep hill. There was barely time for her to brake and manoeuvre the large car to the side of the road, and she sat in stunned disbelief as the driver of the

other car flashed past her, either not realising or
not caring how nearly he had caused an accident.
Once she had recovered a little Saffron tried to
turn the Rolls back on to the road, but the back
wheels slid helplessly on the snow. With a sinking
feeling she realised that she wasn't going to be able
to move it, and worse, the car was slowly slipping
backwards down the hill. Pulling on the brake, she
climbed out to survey her situation, her heart
plummeting downwards as she realised that she
was going to have to leave the Rolls and walk
back to the house on foot.

At least she could make her phone call to the
London office asking them to let her father know
where she was. She could also ring the local garage
to get them to come out and tow the Rolls away.

Still shaken from the close brush with the other
car, she walked to the phone box, searching in her
purse for change.

She picked up the receiver, frowning when there
was no reassuring purr, but it was only after she
had jiggled the buttons up and down several times
that she realised that this phone, like the one up at
the house, was out of order. Thoroughly cross, cold
and tired, she collected her shopping from the car
and started to walk, not along the road, but cutting
across the fields, knowing it would save her time.

She had dressed casually for her drive to the
village—cord jeans, fashion boots, a fur jacket her
father had bought her the previous Christmas;
attractive and warm clothes for shopping in
Knightsbridge, but hardly protection enough for a
cross-country hike in below-zero temperatures,
and before she had covered even half the distance
her feet were numb, her legs aching from the
unaccustomed exercise. The icy wind that had

sprung up chilled her face, and her expensive leather mittens did nothing to protect her fingers, and yet despite her discomfort she plodded determinedly on, until at last the stone wall surrounding the gardens of the house came into sight. She let herself in via a small door in the wall and trudged tiredly round to the back door.

The house felt blissfully warm after the cold outside, and she went upstairs to run herself a bath, trying the telephone once more before she took her purchases into the kitchen. The phone was still dead, and Saffron bit her lip. At least the Rolls wasn't likely to be a hazard to any other traffic using the road, and Bart, her boss, knew she was down here. Poor Daddy, the Rolls was his pride and joy, she only hoped the phone would be fixed in time for her to rescue it before he returned from New York. The walk had given her an appetite; and for the first time since the trial she found she was actually enjoying the thought of food—but first a warming bath!

There was a forgotten bottle of bath oil in the cupboard and she poured it generously into the water, watching it turn pale green and foam. The water enveloped her in a warm, perfumed cloud, and she relaxed into it, shivering as her body remembered against her will how she had felt when Nico touched her, how her body had yielded and responded. No matter how much she tried to force herself to forget, the memories refused to die. She towelled her skin roughly, hoping to dispel the sensuality rising up inside her, then wandered into her bedroom to collect clean clothes. She pulled open a drawer which revealed neatly folded summer tops put there after her holiday in the Caribbean, her attention suddenly caught and held by the masculine shape of a cotton shirt. Slowly she unfolded it, staring at it, as memories flooded back. It was Nico's shirt. She had found it in her room after they had made love, and put it on. She lifted it to her face, holding it as though it still retained the scent and feel of his body, hers an aching mass of pain. Before she could deny herself the pleasure she pulled it on. It drowned her, but she didn't care. It had belonged to Nico; he had worn it. She was just brushing her hair when she heard someone banging on the front door.

For a moment surprise held her frozen, then she put down the brush and hurried to the stairs, forgetting that she was still wearing the shirt, her legs long and slender beneath the tails. Someone had probably driven past, seen lights on and knowing the house should be empty was calling to check that everything was all right. Country people were like that. She opened the door, the reassuring words dying on her lips as her father shouldered his way past her, brushing snowflakes from his coat, his face tired and drawn, as he paused and then turned, speaking to the man still emerging from the car parked in front of the house.

'It's okay, Dom,' she heard him call. 'She's here, and safe . . . God, Saffron, when we saw the Rolls I nearly had a heart attack!'

'But, Daddy, what are you doing here? How did you know . . .'

'Dom rang me from London to say that he'd called at the penthouse and you weren't there. He rang Bart, who told him that you were coming down here. I was already on my way back, so we drove down together. I tried to ring you and couldn't get through.' His eyes rested soberly on her face and Saffron had no need to ask why he had driven all the way down to Surrey simply because he couldn't raise her on the phone. His anxiety and grief was etched all over his face.

'Oh, Daddy!' Her voice suddenly became tart as she glanced towards the still open front door. 'Your friend Dom seems to have been very busy— couldn't he simply accept Bart's word for it that I was down here?'

'Oh, don't blame Dom,' her father told her. 'I asked him to keep an eye on you. I must say when I saw the Rolls . . .'

'Mmm, I was hoping to recover it before you got back.' Briefly Saffron explained what had happened. There were sounds of activity from outside and she realised that all she had on was a man's shirt, decent enough perhaps, but overtly sexy for all that, and she hurried towards the stairs, not wanting to be caught in such garb by her father's friend.

She didn't make it. She had just reached the first step when she heard the door slam, and her father saying in a curiously strained voice,

'It's okay, Dom, she's fine.'

'I'm relieved to hear it.'

So cool and formal—and yet she knew that voice as well as she knew her own. She turned on the stairs, her face as white as her borrowed shirt, her lips trying to form a name and yet trembling so much that all she could manage was a stifled protest before a roaring black void swallowed her up as she heard her father exclaiming anxiously, 'I should have warned her... prepared her, but I was so terrified that she'd done something silly...' and then there was nothing, nothing but darkness, and a fear that she must be going mad, because the man her father had called 'Dom' was surely Nico. Nico who was dead; Nico who had kidnapped and humiliated her; Nico whom she loved; Nico, who simply could not be a man called Dom who watched her with cold dark eyes and wore a formal business suit much like her father's, his dark hair smoothed into order, his mouth impatient and angry.

'Daddy?'

'He's gone—back to London.'

Nico! So it hadn't been a dream! Saffron opened her eyes slowly. She was lying on her own bed in her father's house, everything familiar and safe; everything but the man leaning against the window, his face in shadow, his stance poised and alert.

'I think it's time you and I had a talk.'

Hysteria welled up inside her. He had let her think he was dead; he had masqueraded as her father's friend; he had made love to her and broken her heart, and now he thought they should talk!

She turned away from him, hunching her shoulders childishly.

'Don't speak to me!'

She felt rather than heard him move, surefooted and electrically male as he came to stand beside the bed. She wished he had not come to stand beside her, it made her feel vulnerable; it made her remember . . . She watched the hand he stretched out towards her in horrified revulsion, her bitter 'Don't touch me!' jerked past trembling lips. 'Don't touch me,' she breathed huskily. 'Don't come near me. I hate you!'

'Do you?' He dropped down on his haunches so that their eyes were on a level. Saffron tried to sit upright, but his arm across her shoulders kept her pinned to the bed.

'Is that why you're wearing my shirt; why you wanted to save my life, why you told your father you wished you had conceived my child?' he demanded emotively.

She tried to swallow and found she couldn't. 'Daddy can't have told you that,' she moaned. 'He would never . . .'

'He told me.' The flat words possessed an undeniable ring of truth. 'Are you going to tell me you lied to him?'

Saffron ignored the question. 'Who are you?'

'You know who I am,' he said tersely, 'Dominic Hunter, godson of your father's best friend. And you still haven't answered my question.'

'You haven't answered mine.'

'In this game as in all others, might gives right, so tell me, did you mean what you said to your father?'

'Yes.' The word was dragged painfully out of her. 'But I didn't mean it about you,' she threw at him, 'I meant it about a man who doesn't exist.'

'He exists all right.' Would you like me to prove it to you?'

'No!' She recoiled, and he laughed bitterly.

'Some love if it makes you react like that. Perhaps I ought to remind you of just how easily that hatred you're pushing at me right now can be turned into something very different.

'What are you doing here?' Saffron demanded. 'I don't understand . . .'

'What's the matter?' he jeered unkindly. 'Has all the romance gone out of it now that you know the truth, now that you've discovered that I'm just a man like any other, and not some fictional hero? You don't know the first thing about love, little girl; you're still living in a fantasy world.'

He turned suddenly, getting to his feet and

walking across to the window, his back to her, his hands thrust into the pockets of the expensive suit he was wearing.

'I came here today because your father asked me to. He's been worried about you; worried that you . . .'

'Were pining away for love of a man he knew didn't exist?' Saffron said bitterly, swinging her feet to the floor.

'It was something neither of us had bargained for. Look,' Dominic said quietly, 'either we sit down and I tell you the way it was, or I walk out of here and leave you nurturing all that hatred and bitterness you're so intent on clinging on to— which is it to be?'

'You're going to tell me the truth?'

He turned round to face her, and she saw what she had not seen before—that he looked older, tireder, that something had been stamped on to his features that had not been there before.

'Are you woman enough to hear it?'

Saffron only hesitated for a moment. No matter what pain it might bring her she owed it to herself to face facts.

'Yes,' she said firmly.

'It all started eighteen months ago. My parents died when I was in my teens and my godfather more or less brought me up. We were very close; he was exceptionally good to me, a deeply caring and understanding man. The intention was that I would take over his legal practice from him and that he would semi-retire—he was a keen fisherman and he was looking forward to having more time to spend on his favourite hobby. That was why he went to Italy in the first place. I was to have gone with him, but at the last minute there was a problem at work. I'd run a bit wild in my teens after I lost my parents—in fact I ran away from school and joined the Army—crazy thing to do, but it taught me things about life I would never have learned otherwise. My godfather stood by me and I wanted to repay him, to make him feel that he could trust the practice to me, so he went to Italy alone—and never came back.' His eyes were bitter and Saffron felt his pain, against her will.

'While he was over there he was kidnapped; I got the ransom demand, but the amount they wanted was more than I could raise quickly. I did my best—played it their way; eventually managed to raise the money with some help from your father, but it was all too late.'

'They killed him,' Saffron guessed.

'Yes. I tried to get the Italian authorities to do something, but they were worse than useless, so I decided to take matters into my own hands. When I was in the Army, I was with the . . .'

'The S.A.S.?' Saffron supplied.

'Yes. So I decided to see if I could infiltrate the gang—the Italian authorities knew who they were, they just couldn't touch them—too clever for them—so I followed them and watched them, got to know as much about the organisation as I could. I was aided by the fact that each unit worked virtually independently of the main organisation. I knew it wouldn't be impossible to infiltrate—to pretend as I eventually did that I'd been sent by the organisation to work with them. All I needed was a tempting enough piece of bait.'

'Me?'

'I discussed it with your father and assured him that you would be quite safe.' He grimaced slightly. 'What I hadn't bargained for was that . . .'

'I would be stupid enough to fall in love with you?' Saffron supplied bitterly.

He turned to face her, his expression unreadable. 'Did you? I thought the name of the game was a little sexual experimentation; a little living before the cup of life was snatched away. No, what I hadn't bargained for was that you weren't the sophisticated woman I'd been led to expect from the press, but a halfbaked innocent who didn't know the first thing about protecting herself.'

'So you did it for me?' Bitterness and disillusionment mingled in the words. 'By deceiving me, terrifying me and seducing me?'

'Acquit me of the last one,' he told her cruelly. 'You were with me all the way, however you try to disguise your motives now. Anyway,' he went on, 'I protected you as best I could without alerting the others.'

'All those trips into the town?' Saffron queried. 'They were to . . .'

'Report back to your father, and pass information on to my back-up team.'

'Fellow members of the S.A.S.?' Saffron suggested, the whole thing becoming clearer by the minute.

'Yes, acting in an unofficial capacity and with the agreement of the Italian authorities.'

'How did you manage to infiltrate the gang in the first place?' Saffron asked. 'By becoming Olivia's lover?'

'No?' A muscle jerked in his jaw. 'But if I had done, would I have been any worse than you?' he asked roughly. 'And don't tell me you weren't hoping to persuade me to set you free, or that it didn't ever cross your mind.'

Suddenly they were two strangers facing one

another across a deep chasm of mutual bitterness. Saffron knew why she was bitter and resentful, but why was he? Because her father had insisted on him coming to see her; because he simply didn't want any further involvement with her and feared it might be forced on him?

'What I can't understand is my father,' she began unsteadily, but Dominic cut across her words.

'I asked him to say nothing; and besides, like me, he believed you were "in love" with the idea of being in love; I told you, the enforced intimacy of such a situation causes strange things. What neither he or I bargained for was . . .'

'That Guido would try to rape me and I would fling myself at you because of it?' Saffron said quietly. 'Well, neither your nor Daddy need feel embarrassed about the possibility of a repeat performance.'

It hurt her more than she wanted to admit to know that everything that had happened had been calculated and planned for; that all he had wanted was to be avenged on his godfather's murderers, that she had simply been a helpless pawn.

'You do realise that your father thought you'd killed yourself when he saw the car, don't you?' he said flatly. 'To say nothing of what I felt.'

'Delight, I expect,' Saffron said bitterly. 'How embarrassing for you to be landed with my unwanted feelings! What's the matter, is Daddy putting pressure on you to make an honest woman out of me? Well, don't worry about it—I wouldn't want you now if you were the last man on earth!'

She turned her back on him, flinching in shock as he crossed the floor silently, grasping her arms and forcing her round to face him.

'Want to bet on that one?' he asked her

cynically. The colour rose and fell in her face, her breathing suddenly constricted as he lowered his head and touched her lips with his. It took every ounce of willpower she possessed to resist the mad impulse to fling her arms round his neck, to hold him and beg him to make love to her, to love her as she loved him. Still loved him, she acknowledged—nothing had changed that, not knowing how he had deceived, not learning that he didn't give a damn for her, not anything, but at least she had enough pride left to keep her lips hard and unresponsive beneath the angry scorch of his, although why was he doing this to her, unless it was some crazy form of punishing?

When at last Dominic raised his head his eyes were almost black and undecipherable. Saffron's nails had left tiny crescents of pain where she had pressed them into her palms, her whole body tense with the effort of maintaining an outward show of indifference.

'Are you going now?' she asked unpleasantly, marvelling at her ability to appear unmoved when inside her she was crying with pain and hurt.

'Not just yet.' There was silky menace in the words, something about the determination in his eyes that sent danger signals flooding through her body. She looked wildly at the door, but to reach it she would have to brush past him, and there was no way she was going to allow her body to come into contact with his voluntarily.

'You've still got something that belongs to me, I believe.' He looked pointedly down at the shirt she was wearing.

'This? You want this?'

'Not only want but am going to have,' he promised softly, and bent towards her. Saffron

thought he was going to start unfastening the
buttons and clutched the lapels protectively, eyes
huge in her fragile face, but to her shock he simply
grasped the edges and pulled roughly, buttons
flying in one direction while the shirt gaped open,
exposing her body to his gaze.

'You want it?' Her voice was shrill with temper
and fear, as she slid the shirt off her body, driven
beyond anger or embarrassment, to a pitch of fury
she had never experienced before. Not caring that
she was completely naked apart from the tiny lace
briefs she was wearing, she rolled the torn shirt
into a ball and flung it at him. 'Then take it . . .
Take it and get out, and don't ever come back!'

He fielded the shirt almost absently, his eyes
fastened on her body, a look in them that made
her heart begin a hurried drumbeat of spiralling
panic.

'You can't imagine the torment of remembering
you like this and not being able to do a damned
thing about it,' he told her hoarsely. 'Night after
night, day after day, until I thought I was going to
go crazy, that I *was* crazy, no woman could be so
perfect, so desirable, but I was wrong.'

Saffron moved, and his hands jerked out, fingers
biting into the soft flesh of her waist.

'Even now you don't know what we had, do
you?' he said slowly. 'How rare what happened
between us was; so rare that I've never experienced
it before and never want to again. That first night
in Rome . . .'

A terrible pain seemed to explode inside her,
sending shivering fragments of anguish into every
part of her body.

'Why?'

'Because I can't experience it again and live

through the knowledge that that's all it is—one experience. I want it for ever; I want you for ever. It tears me apart to think of any other man touching you, seeing you, like this.'

It was some new refined form of torture he'd devised especially for her, Saffron thought numbly, it had to be.

'Let me go ... Let me go!' she told him fiercely.

'Not until I've done this.'

'This' was a kiss that inflamed her to the point where she couldn't think of anything but the need to feel his body next to hers.

'I know you can't really love me,' she heard him whisper against her throat. 'You don't even know me, but wanting you and not having you is driving me mad; I can't think straight, ever since they let me out of hospital...'

'Hospital?' she stiffened in his arms.

'You don't surely think I wouldn't have come to you before if I could? I told myself you were just experimenting, just growing up, that I was a fool to read anything serious into it, but I was bewitched. When I thought of Guido touching you I wanted to tear him limb from limb. I couldn't forgive myself for exposing you to him—for what so nearly happened. You were so frightened, so ... I nearly went mad when you begged me to take you! I told myself I wasn't going to, but the first touch of your body beneath my hands, your lips on my skin...'

'I thought you didn't want me because I was a virgin.'

'Like hell!' Dominic murmured succinctly. 'I wanted you all right; from the very first moment I set eyes on you, there was a very special magic between us from the very first, but it wasn't until I saw how courageous you were, how brave despite your fear, and how appallingly innocent, that I realised I loved you as well, and hated myself for the danger I'd brought to you. I underestimated your effect on Guido—and myself. There were times when I came close to calling the whole thing off, but I couldn't without exposing you to further danger.'

'You love me?' She frowned as he winced, suddenly remembering what he had said about hospital. 'They told me you were dead,' she whispered, filled with the horror of that moment.

'So that Guido, Olivia and their friends wouldn't come looking for me—a very natural precaution, and one your father fully endorsed until after the trial and you told him the truth. He gave me some pretty gruelling moments, I can tell you, despite my wounds. I was in hospital at the time recovering from the gunshot wound Olivia inflicted.'

'When you saved my life,' Saffron murmured brokenly. 'I was going to tell them that at the trial. I was going to . . .'

'I know all about that,' Dominic said grimly. 'Hell, you really know how to put a man through it, don't you?'

'I told Daddy I loved you, and even then he said nothing.' There was pain in her voice and eyes.

'What could he do? We both thought you were suffering from a severe case of infatuation—it isn't exactly uncommon in the circumstances.' He grimaced slightly, flexing a shoulder, and Saffron remembered that he wasn't long out of hospital. 'You think *you* had problems. I knew what I felt was no infatuation, but I promised your father I'd give you time to adjust to normal life again, and anyway, being in hospital hardly meant that I could sweep you off your feet, but I was getting to the stage where even if he hadn't come to see me, I was coming to see you. Can you imagine how I felt when I reached the penthouse and discovered you'd left! I'd got it all planned, quiet dinner somewhere, plus explanations, and then...'

'Then what?' Saffron asked huskily, hardly daring to let herself hope.

'Then a night of bliss in my arms,' Dominic said softly, 'after which you'd be in no fit state to refuse my offer of making an honest woman out of you. There at least I was on safe ground. I knew how you would respond to me. Hell, I spent long enough trying to forget! I knew it was taking an unfair advantage, you were hardly in a position to make comparisons, but I'd reached the stage where I was desperate enough to use any means of keeping you in my life. I told myself I'd just have to convince you that what we had was pretty special and that infatuation or not, I intended to become a permanent feature in your life. Even to the extent of using blackmail if need be.'

'Blackmail?' Saffron looked puzzled, and he laughed, drawing her down into his arms.

'Yes, my lovely little wanton; that child you so badly wanted to conceive.'

'You mean...'

'I mean I love you so damn much I'd even descend to the level of making you pregnant to make sure you married me.'

'I thought that was my role,' Saffron dimpled, laughing as he rolled over and pulled her down on top of him, kissing the laughter from her mouth, his fingers caressing her breasts until they peaked into hard arousal, and she heard him groan protestingly against her skin.

'Where you're concerned I lose all self-control. I want you, Saffron; I love you and I need you.'

'I love you too,' she whispered back, 'so much that I can't wait to fall asleep at night and dream that you're with me.' A faint blush coloured her skin, and he laughed triumphantly.

'I can do better than that, my love—much, much better, but only if you promise to make an honest man of me just as soon as it can be arranged; otherwise I'll tell our grandchildren how you seduced me.'

Saffron laughed, loving him more than ever in this teasing mood, but the laughter died from her eyes when she looked up at him and saw the love she had longed for so achingly, her body trembling as she arched beneath him, his groaned response smothered against her skin as his mouth moved from her lips to her breast and back again.

This time there was no need for him to beg her to undress him, nor to make allowances for her inexperience, nor indeed any need for Saffron to dam up the husky words of love she murmured against his skin, eliciting an instantaneous response. Dominic loved her and she loved him, and she could forgive him all deceit, all pain, everything—because he had given her so much already in compensation, and that, as he told her in the aftermath of their lovemaking, was just the beginning. The best was yet to come!

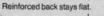